ALIEN STARS

Book 3 of the Harry Stubbs Adventures

by David Hambling

Macabre Ink

Three men waited outside one of the sheds. Two had armed themselves with gardening forks and stood ready to repel whatever was inside. Their attitude suggested it might be a bear, wolf, or other dangerous animal.

"What's the situation, sir?" asked Skinner.

Stafford ran a hand through his hair before answering. "It's the under-gardener, Pierce." The tremor in his voice signified a man trapped in a nightmare. "He has lost his mind. We've cornered him in the shed here, but he won't come out."

"And you require some assistance in restraining your under-gardener," said Skinner as though we were dealing with no more than an escaped rabbit. "I take it he is displaying signs of violence?"

"Some signs." Stafford raised the shotgun almost apologetically. It was a fine weapon with filigree work around the barrel. "This is only birdshot to keep him back if he turns dangerous. Just to be safe."

"I see." Skinner turned to the younger of the servants. "You run along now, sonny, and fetch us a couple of pairs of thick gloves—one medium-sized, the other the biggest you've got—at least two lengths of decent rope, and a canvas bag big enough to put over his head. Quick as you can, now! We'll see he doesn't get out while you're gone."

The boy stood his fork against a greenhouse and hurried off while Skinner and I removed our jackets.

"What would you like us to do with your under-gardener once he's restrained?" asked Skinner.

For Pip

ISBN 978-1-948929-74-5

For information address Crossroad Press at 141 Brayden Dr., Hertford, NC 27944
A Macabre Ink Production - Macabre Ink is an imprint of Crossroad Press.
www.crossroadpress.com

First edition

The gull shall whistle in his wake, the blind wave break in fire.
He shall fulfil God's utmost will, unknowing his desire,
And he shall see old planets change and alien stars arise.

Rudyard Kipling, "The Voortrekker"

When I was writing *Pan* and *The White Powder* I did not believe that such strange things had ever happened in real life, or could ever have happened. Since then, and quite recently, I have had certain experiences in my own life which have entirely changed my point of view in these matters.

Arthur Machen, Letter to Paul-Jean Touletin

Special thanks to Carly Randall, Archivist at the Horniman Museum, for her invaluable assistance and patience above and beyond.

Preamble

If you are reading this document, then I shall be dead.

Latham and Rowe, a firm that I know to be trustworthy, has instructions not to release my papers until I have been legally judged to be deceased. I expect they will have explained this to you, but I wanted to be clear about it and also about my reasons for writing this narrative.

It was not my idea but Skinner's and occurred when I told him about the written accounts of my previous activities. Skinner is a sharp chap—none sharper, in my opinion—and though not one for writing himself, he suggested this measure to me. His notion is that this document will leave so many clues as to make it impossible to do away with us without the guilty party being brought to justice—the idea being that because of the insurance policy, nobody would take the risk.

I will attempt to write matters up as they occur. As I write up each new section, I will deliver it to Latham and Rowe to be added, unopened and unseen, to the collection. Of course, in the event of my untimely demise, this story may be an unfinished one that you will have to complete yourself. If this is the case, I apologise to the reader for the inconvenience—though such an occurrence will be a deal more inconvenient for me than for you.

Also, if my presumed death is not sufficient warning, I am duty bound to advise you that these are dangerous matters. By reading this, you are putting yourself in some degree of peril, the reasons for which cannot be explained briefly and will become apparent in the following pages.

You may find much of what follows hard to credit. Not long

ago, I would have agreed with you. But if you have seen the accounts of my earlier cases—now also lodged with Latham and Rowe for safekeeping—you will appreciate how my view of the world has altered in the past year.

The world is not as I thought it was. My process of discovery is a continuing one. It is not so much like discovering the South Pole or climbing a mountain. It is more like exploring a series of caverns and finding that at the end of each there is an entrance into another deeper, darker cavity where the rock formations are even more unpleasantly suggestive and where the markings on the walls lead ever farther into the abyssal depths. These caves are not uninhabited.

I am beginning to feel that these preliminary explanations and qualifications will only add to your confusion rather than dispelling it. Therefore, it is best that I conclude this introduction without more ado and proceed to business. And if you do decide to read on, I thank you for taking my side. Skinner is a good man to have in my corner, but as I know from my boxing days, it makes all the difference in the world to have spectators at the ringside cheering you on.

Chapter One

The Thing in Room Eight

I will skip some weeks of preliminaries and start at the point where Skinner and I were given our first significant assignment.

Skinner had been working on his own for a few months before I joined him. He was vague about his occupation since the war. He had served in the Fusiliers with some distinction, being involved in several notable actions, and his record made my time in the Royal Artillery look like a cakewalk. He had lost the taste for any kind of settled job after that. Working with Skinner felt like army life turned bandit, with more emphasis on loafing and looting than soldiering.

In the first weeks of my employment, our tasks were more in the nature of training exercises or manoeuvres than actual operations. We had daily and weekly schedules of tasks to be carried out. For example, we had to check whether a certain tomb in West Norwood Cemetery had been disturbed, look for the presence of certain articles in the lists published by auction houses, and read for mention of certain individuals in the local press.

Sometimes we had to follow a person or keep an eye on a building for a set period of time and note the comings and goings therefrom. Skinner called this "playing at spies."

We also had more curious chores, such as renewing chalk marks on certain walls. The exact significance of the marks was never explained to us. Like good soldiers, we followed instructions to the letter.

The job had some of the sense of army life about it, of the seemingly purposeless ritual activity that nevertheless had a hidden motivation. I do not know why they always set you to painting all the stones white in an army camp, but it did have some psychic effect on the occupants of the base. And perhaps that was the main function of these tasks—to remind us what we were about and keep our minds focused.

Such assignments were not generally enough to keep Skinner and me occupied the entire day, but we were obliged to put in the hours and to be on call in case we were needed. Plenty of those summer afternoons found us sitting in the office, Skinner idly reading out snippets from the newspaper or working his way through the crossword puzzle while I worked away at a correspondence course. Skinner found the idea of learning to be a private detective by post highly comical, but then, he had little respect for any form of book learning. I would never learn to break into a house, or how to bribe an official, from a book. Perhaps that sort of business was better learned while on duty with a suitable police force, but I did pick up some useful tips during my studies.

The name of our employer was never to be spoken out loud. While strictly speaking there was nothing illegal about our activities, he treated us as a guilty secret. You would think he was concealing a mistress rather than an interest in matters that went beyond respectable science.

The pay was more than generous. My stock of good shirts and collars increased. A quiet evening drinking with a friend was not a luxury, and I could enjoy nights out at the Conquering Hero without fretting about buying a round. I was happy to be tapped for loans as more of my friends found themselves laid off or working reduced hours. I could afford a good seat at the pictures whenever I wanted, and I was able to replace my old, worn-out kit at the boxing gym.

My biggest extravagance was books. I did not take the opportunity to stock up on the great classics, I am ashamed to say. A person cannot always be bettering himself. I built up my own little library of good shilling editions—cheaply bound versions of popular novels. With my new income, I could pick up Kipling or Rider Haggard or Buchan whenever I felt like it. We were living, as Skinner liked to say, on Easy Street in the land of milk and honey.

Skinner is notionally my superior, having been in this employment a few months longer than me. He is an easy-going type, and working with him is not burdensome. Some might say he is too easy-going. He is the only man I know who smokes Blue Box, the ones with a mix of Russian, Turkish, Egyptian, and Havana mix cigarettes. Perhaps that says something about his restless spirit.

Skinner was briefly taken on by my friend and patron Arthur Renville, whose trade in consignments of goods occupies a lucrative grey area between legal and illegal and involves many individuals with no regular employment. Arthur was not pleased with Skinner's efforts and suggested that a day's hard work would probably kill him. Skinner cheekily replied that this sounded like a good enough reason to avoid hard work. Arthur has not found need for Skinner's services since, but had recommended him to our current employer

Now, Skinner and I had been assigned the task of confronting a woman he had traced to a rooming house in Sydenham. As per our usual procedure, he gave me a short briefing. Standing side by side, we might have been part of a sketch from a Charlie Chaplin film. Skinner would be Chaplin, the comedic tramp, always with one eye out for a pretty girl; I'd be Eric Campbell, the enormous bully who smashed things up and chased him around the set. Of course, Campbell came out worse in the end, but he was always back for the next encounter. Or at least until his untimely death in 1917.

"I've only seen her properly once," said Skinner. "She's calling herself Mabel Brown, which may be an alias. She's probably somewhere between twenty and thirty years of age, medium height, slim build, and with short brown hair that is shingled. Not a bad-looking girl, either, as far as I could tell."

"Do we have any information about this item we're meant to be retrieving?"

"Not a dicky bird." Skinner turned the paper over to see if there was anything on the other side and gave me the conspiratorial smile of an NCO to his squad in the face of poor direction from his superiors. "They're sending us in blind. But are we downhearted?"

"No, no, no!" I gave the traditional army response, which was both expected and merited.

"I dare say we will be able to improvise. As per usual." Skinner made it sound simple. He never lacked confidence. He possessed what the French called *savoir faire*. I envied his way of adapting himself to any situation. All too often, I felt like an actor without a script arriving halfway through a scene. Skinner had lines at his fingertips for every situation; others thought they knew where they were until he confused them with his ad-libbing.

"It's like a dance," he said, seeing my troubled look. "Neither you nor I know what this is about, as the powers that be have not seen fit to enlighten us. But this Mabel Brown knows. When she sees us, she'll know the game is up. She'll lead us in a dance, and whether she waltzes or foxtrots, we'll match her step for step."

Skinner was an old hand in the dance halls, but I have never been a dancer. People would laugh at me if I tried. But I understood the gist. Skinner's plan was that he would loiter near the rooming house and follow Mabel Brown when she emerged. I would be waiting by the bus stop at the far end of the street. When I saw him follow a woman, I was to step out, and then the two of us would confront her so she could not easily get away.

"She won't scream or cry out," he said. "The last thing she wants is a scene and the police being called. But we'll have to be careful."

"Do you think she might be dangerous?"

"Women are always dangerous," Skinner said, patting me on the arm. He considered himself an expert on the fairer sex, having—he said—carried out extensive research in the field. And numerous other places.

We moved off to our allotted posts. Skinner could loiter anywhere without attracting attention; he was a born loafer. He was one of those types you saw propping up walls or leaning on lampposts, providing a running commentary to each other on the comings and goings on the street. Skinner could push his hat back, adopt an attitude, and look as though he had been a fixture since the street was built. Nobody looked twice at him.

Sydenham was a prosperous suburb inhabited by working people, and there was a steady stream of folks on their way to work or queuing politely behind me at the bus stop.

I perused the posters, feeling that my physique again put me at a disadvantage. I did not have the knack of hanging around, even at a bus stop where people might linger by rights. Self-consciousness had much to do with it. What with my size, the broken nose, and my general demeanour, people gave me looks, and that made me awkward. I never knew what to do with my hands. The more I tried to keep out of sight, the more furtive I appeared. Even standing there, reading about the attractions at the funfair coming to Streatham Common— "Death-Defying Displays of Acrobatic Prowess! Entertainment for Young and Old! Prize Contests of Skill and Chance!"—I sensed passers-by steering around me.

After an interminable period, during which buses came and went and people passed by, Skinner ambled up. "She's late. Just like a woman. Let's go in and confront her."

"You mean knocking on the door?"

"No. Breaking and entering. Are you game, Bombardier?"

For two men to break into an occupied house in broad daylight was lunacy, but Skinner was nothing if not daring. I did not need to tell him that if anybody decided to call the police, we would be sunk. I had neither aptitude nor experience as a cat burglar. But as the saying goes, fortune favours the brave.

"Yes, Sergeant," I said.

"Good man!" He slapped my shoulder. "Walk this way. It's a sad day when two bachelors as eligible as you and me have to break into a ladies' rooming house. Normally, I can find an obliging damsel to let me in the back door... but we're in a hurry, and needs must."

The rooming house was a four-storey affair of red brick, built as a family home in the last century when people had troops of servants rather than just one or two. There was a main entrance at the front and a side entrance for deliveries down a sort of alley. In that alley, Skinner had spotted that one of the windows that followed the staircase up the side of the house had been left open a couple of inches. It was eight feet above the ground.

We strolled in as though approaching the side entrance. Without being asked, I formed a stirrup with my hands and boosted Skinner up. Steadying himself with one hand on a drainpipe, he struggled with the window.

"Can you manage a tad higher?" he whispered.

It was no great feat for me to lift him first to chest height, then up to shoulder height, and finally high above my head.

"Wa-hey," said Skinner. "The Flying Bonzini Brothers are in town! Going up. Second floor, ladies' undergarments, here we go…"

It was an awkward piece of gymnastics, but the window latch clicked as Skinner worked the mechanism, and in a second his weight lifted from my hands. He appeared at the window and, by dumb show, indicated that I was to go to the side door. I was hardly there before it opened.

I passed him his hat and briefcase.

"Thank you kindly," he whispered then ushered me in. "Welcome to no man's land."

There was a clatter of cutlery and crockery from the kitchen, where someone must have been washing up, but no other sign of life. Keeping quiet, as our male voices would attract instant attention, we made our way to the front hall. Skinner scanned the letters laid out on the hall table.

You could tell it was a ladies' rooming house. Like a men's rooming house, there was a background smell of boiled cabbage, but here it was masked by sweeter, feminine scents of powder and perfume and fancy soaps. Cigarettes and the less pleasant male odours were absent. A stand by the door held half a dozen dainty umbrellas and a couple of parasols, and there were no dirty boots. Every surface sprouted little china knick-knacks, the sort that would last five minutes with even sober men tramping through.

Skinner found a letter in the pile addressed to Mabel Brown

and slipped it into an inner pocket while I struggled to make sense of the guest book. A gramophone played in one of the downstairs rooms. The swirling tones of Midnight Waltz added to the unreal quality and highlighted my impression of being in a different world.

I held up eight fingers and gestured towards the staircase to signify that Mabel Brown was in room eight. We tiptoed upstairs like thieves. I was still imagining the embarrassment I would feel if someone found us there, when Skinner pointed to a door bearing a porcelain shield with painted irises and the number eight.

He turned the handle stealthily; the door opened at his push. Skinner stepped in briskly, and I was right behind him. I half expected a scream, but there was no sound.

The room was empty.

I closed the door noiselessly behind me.

"Where is she?" whispered Skinner, and I shrugged.

If Mabel Brown had left, she had not troubled to lock the door behind her, and there were no signs of flight—no drawers left open or items scattered around.

Skinner scratched his head and looked at his watch. "She must still be in the house. See that? The key's still in the door. She's either in the bathroom or closeted with her landlady downstairs. Very well; it gives us a chance to search the place."

"What are we looking for?"

"You'll know it when you find it," he said.

The room was a comfortable size and made bigger because the furniture was so sparse—a single bed against one wall, a chest of drawers that was also the bedside table, a chair, a folding table, a shelf of books, and a washstand with a mirror. There was no wardrobe, but an alcove had been curtained off for the purpose. The small fireplace was decorated with a spray of dried flowers in place of a fire for the summer.

The room retained an odour of smoke. There was no ashtray, and I doubted whether smoking would be permitted in a ladies' guesthouse. Perhaps Mabel Brown was not a well-behaved young lady and liked the odd furtive cigarette.

We searched in complete silence while the Midnight Waltz

played again below us. The neighbours had to be tired of hearing the same tunes played on the gramophone over and over.

It fell to me to search the alcove. There were coats and dresses hanging up and a pile of hatboxes and cases on the floor. One of those proved to contain a pair of roller skates, which brought to mind the young women who swished around the skating rink at the Crystal Palace of a Saturday. My ma called them flappers and did not approve one bit, but I could not help wondering whether Mabel Brown was pretty and if she skated well.

Skinner, meanwhile, went through the chest of drawers and paused to pick through a jewellery box. "What a lot of rubbish," he whispered disgustedly, poking at a brooch shaped like a teddy bear. "She never wears any of these, and now it's so full she can't find any of the good ones."

"They're memories," I said, wondering if Sherlock Holmes could reconstruct her history from the contents of her jewellery box and tell us who Mabel Brown really was.

Skinner had already crammed the trinkets back and was rifling through a drawer of perfume bottles and jars and little boxes.

A shelf by the bed held an alarm clock, a small lamp, and a book—a Western romance, *The Prairie Bride*. The bookmark was a folded sheet of printed paper with some handwriting in pencil. The printed text was a recipe for ragout of wild duck, but I was more interested in the jotted notes:

Archivist, janitor (?), master (?)—held where??

EG protection—Lock pick/chisel

Poss. New England 1882?

I folded the paper and slipped it in my pocket, hoping to decipher it later.

Under the bed were two cases. I opened the smaller, a battered brown-leather affair. It was full of old magazines, cinema ones mainly, and programs from theatres and concerts but nothing personal. There were no bundles of letters tied with ribbon—nothing, really, to suggest that she had occupied the place for more than a few months.

As I was sliding the suitcase back, I noticed a small, shiny object under the bed. I picked it up to examine it. It was black and no larger than a pea. I thought at first it was a black pearl or some other piece of jewellery that had got loose, but it was soft and not cold to the touch and had the feel of organic matter.

"Bile bean," said Skinner, looking over my shoulder.

"What?"

"Bile beans. Women love 'em. Helps them to stay slim. Must have dropped it."

Another of those things you did not learn in correspondence courses. Not knowing what else to do, I put the thing back down where I had found it.

"Well, that's a bust," said Skinner.

"Loose floorboard?" I whispered, recalling the Shackleton case. The carpet stopped a good six inches from the wall. I checked the state of the boards all up and down and found nothing.

I wanted to tell Skinner that he ought to be better at finding female hiding places. He had four sisters but no brothers. Growing up in such an environment left him very much at ease with the gentle sex in all of its manifestations. It should have given him a better understanding of the sorts of hiding places that would appeal to the feminine mind. But it was difficult to strike the right tone of remonstration in whispered conversation, so I applied myself to the problem.

Under the loose floorboards—that was a man's idea. Women would not grope down through dust and cobwebs and maybe mouse nests. Men hid things on inaccessible shelves and behind masonry; women relied on guile and subtly.

That insight seemed of limited use given the absence of hiding places, so I looked at the books along the shelf. A few novels sat on one side, mainly romances but also *Black Oxen, Babbitt, Mrs Dalloway,* and then an interval occupied by two Japanese vases. On the other side was the inevitable Bible, an old copy of *Mrs Beeton's Household Management,* two books of railway timetables, *Flowers of England and Ireland,* and a dozen souvenir theatre programs.

My hand hovered over *Mrs Beeton.* The book was often given away as a school prize but not one that anyone living in a rooming house would have much use for. It was a big, heavy thing to cart around when it could be left at the parental home.

"What about the other case?" Skinner asked.

I could have slapped myself in the forehead, but I wondered if something had made me shy away from opening the larger of the two suitcases under the bed. It was dark leather with big straps and buckles that fastened around it but no lock.

"I've a funny feeling about this," said Skinner, echoing my own thoughts.

Inside the suitcase was a bundle wrapped in a bed sheet. Skinner unrolled it on the floor. As the last fold opened to show its contents, we both froze.

Midnight Waltz played on below.

Skinner and I both had enough presence of mind not to say anything immediately. I heard him taking deep breaths: one, two, three, four. Both of us were staring fixedly at the thing he had just unwrapped.

"There's nothing we can do here," he said quietly. "And there's no point in us being found at the scene. Agreed?"

"Agreed."

Skinner wrapped the bundle up again with quick, jerky movements and shoved it back in the case, which I hastily closed and buckled. He opened the window stealthily and looked down, but there was no prospect of egress in that direction.

"Back door," Skinner said.

I tried hard not to jostle as we hurried down the stairs, the boards creaking with each step, and every second I expected a door to open. Even if someone saw our backs, it would be enough to hang both of us. Our hats were pulled down, and we leaned forward to hide our faces as we came out of the alley and headed down the street.

The image was imprinted on my brain, and I could see it as clearly as a photograph when I closed my eyes. At first the blackened, curled shape had made no sense. Working in a butcher's, I had seen meat in all its shapes and forms, and human bodies were really no different than pigs when you got down to it. This was not meat, though. The crusted, blackened mess did not look like a body at all, not at first. It was curled up like a baby and half the size of a normal adult.

The correct term for the body's condition was "carbonised." The old charcoal burners used to heat wood in fires banked under layers of turf. It did not burn but gradually scorched and charred. The heat slowly drove all the water out. The timber shrank down and became a blackened, desiccated husk in the shape of the original, brittle stuff that left black marks when you touched it.

This shrivelled form had been a human being once. I only knew that when I saw the skull—a withered black citrus rind with two eyeholes looking right at me. Some incredible fire had burned her down to the bones, leaving charcoal sticks for limbs and ribs. But that was not what troubled us most. We had both seen old bones before. What troubled us was the finger—the last two joints of the little finger on the left hand—that was still perfectly intact. It stood out shockingly white against the blackened bones, the nail painted dark red. The skin was fresh, not decayed or even dried. She could not have been dead more than a few hours.

Chapter Two

The Under-Gardener

For our office, we had the use of a room in a mail-order concern dealing in cheap chinaware. The business belonged to a friend of Skinner's, and the operation consisted of nothing more than receiving boxes of wholesale crockery packed in newspaper and making them up into parcels for customers who responded to newspaper advertisements. The number of staff varied from day to day and week to week, but there were generally between four and six women employed there; Skinner's friend showed up on rare occasions to oversee operations but seemed only to slow them down.

The premises were more than the chinaware business needed, so Skinner had leased one of their empty rooms. Our office had only the basic amenities of chairs and a work table along with a battered filing cabinet and chests of china in varying numbers depending on our host's needs. The large window looked out onto a brick wall ten feet away and was partly occluded by a leafy branch, which cast a green shade on the room that was most pleasant on a sunny day. Skinner had brightened the place up with a couple of classical nudes cut from gentleman's magazines.

I might mention that the company that officially occupied the office, and which we officially worked for, was a perfectly genuine operation by the name of Lantern Insurance. Another friend of Skinner's, one who knew about these things, put all the paperwork through Somerset House. If anybody cares to check, Lantern Insurance is a legitimate business, and all our papers are more or less in order.

"This is a turn-up for the books," said Skinner. "We've gone from tiptoeing about, playing games, to full-blown murder enquiry in no time flat."

He stabbed absentmindedly at the desktop with his pocketknife, something he did often enough for the surface to look as though it was afflicted with woodworm.

"A body in a suitcase does suggest murder," I said. "But was it Mabel Brown's body? Or somebody she herself killed?"

"A very pertinent question. I would have said that the cadaver was of a young female, judging by the painted fingernail. So if Mabel Brown is missing, and nobody else from that house is gone, it's got to be her."

We turned that one over, testing it for soundness.

"Or she brought the body into the house in the suitcase," I said, "and disappeared herself."

"The remains were too fresh for that. And I smelled smoke. No, someone killed her and put the remains in the suitcase to avoid detection. If they'd left the body on the floor, the landlady would have found it straight off when she cleaned the room. Packed away like that, it would stay undetected for days. People in the house would think Mabel Brown had just shot the moon and run off."

"But why did the killer leave the suitcase there?"

Skinner shook his head.

"Do you have any notion of how it was done?" I asked.

"Some hocus-pocus," he said darkly. "I didn't see any signs of a conflagration in the room. There hadn't been a fire in the grate for months. It's like they took the body to a crematorium and put the remains in the suitcase."

"A death ray." There was science far beyond our science; I knew that from personal experience. The Martian Heat Ray that H. G. Wells imagined so vividly, which could reduce a man to ashes in moments, was primitive compared to what I had witnessed on an earlier occasion. A memento of that encounter—a ring set with a green stone in the shape of a five-pointed star—hung around my neck. The ring was too small for my finger, but I wore it as a kind of protective talisman. I had reason to believe that its makers predated the human race.

"Who knows?" said Skinner. "But speculation aside, we do have one piece of evidence." He drew from his pocket the envelope he had stolen from the hall table. After examining the outside with a magnifying glass, he slit it open with his knife and flattened the single sheet of writing paper out on the table.

"Female handwriting," he announced then read aloud,

M—

I made enquiries for you last night, and there's a couple of the lads willing to help. They'll want a quid each up front, cash on the nail and no messing about. If it gets rough, they'll want more afterwards, so take some extra with you, but the sight of them should do the trick. They are reliable and will keep their mouths shut after, but don't tell them any more than you have to about your "beetle," or you'll be asking for trouble. Drop me a line, and I'll tip them the wink.

I still can't believe it, but if he pays up like you say, then you can take me with you to Monte Carlo!

E

"Did you say 'beetle'?"

Skinner slid the paper over for me to read for myself.

"The Egyptian scarab beetle has a sacred and magical significance," I said. "Some scarabs made from precious stones are valuable. Apart from that, I can't think of anything."

"Maybe, but *beetle* is in inverted commas, indicating maybe it's not an actual beetle as such. I'm forced to conclude that it is the article we seek, which our lord and master has not seen fit to disclose to us."

"I'll start writing the report," I said.

Writing reports always falls to me; Skinner has no aptitude for the written word, and his penmanship is atrocious. He is a useful source of suggestions, though, and frequently makes observations that I've missed. I have learned a lot from Skinner.

We had completed the first draft, and I was writing it up when one of the girls came with a letter.

"This has just come for Mr Skinner, by a taxi man." She put it on the edge of Skinner's desk with an outstretched arm, as though he might bite, before scuttling out.

"Thank you, my darling," Skinner called after her. He slit the envelope and read quickly. "Oh, dearie me."

"What is it?"

"We are summoned to his Lordship's manse with all haste. The taxicab is waiting outside. If I knew we'd be visiting the quality, I'd have had my valet to lay out a good collar this morning."

Skinner and I had never before been invited to the household of our employer. It had to be for something serious—I had no idea quite how serious.

The Firs is a large property located towards Thornton Heath. If you have only a casual acquaintance with Norwood, you might be forgiven for thinking the area is inhabited entirely by working people who occupy street after street of terraced Victorian houses. Some of the streets are better than others—sometimes the houses grow an extra storey and spread themselves out more, and there are green spaces and brick-built churches—but the real money is largely invisible. There are a surprising number of grand houses tucked away behind rows of trees or down less-used thoroughfares towards Dulwich way. Apparently, back in the old days, long before the Crystal Palace was built, this was a popular area for successful London merchants to build their mansions.

Our employer's home was on one such street of substantial Georgian villas. A high wall enclosed an acre of so of gardens with a row of the eponymous fir trees further screening one side. The house itself could only be seen as you approached the iron gates. The house had a turret, which was not an uncommon embellishment for period residences, but this one was topped with a dome that must have been an astronomical observatory. Mr Stafford was a man of eclectic interests.

A butler was posted outside the gates on the pavement. He briskly unlocked them as our cab approached, which struck me as an unusual procedure. Skinner took a swig from a silver hip flask and offered it to me; I declined. The butler—a gaunt, silver-haired man—directed us, with considerable agitation, to the far end of the garden. He hurried to fasten the gates and return to the house.

We passed flower beds, a small lawn, and a rose garden with a pergola, all in immaculate order. Next, we passed to an area of raised beds then row upon row of seedlings, cold frames, and compost heaps. Seeing backstage made me realise the effort that went into the perfect image up front. Gardens were supposed to mean leisure, but I could see the labour here. As Kipling had it, "better men than we go out and start their working lives / At grubbing weeds from gravel-paths with broken dinner-knives."

We arrived at an arrangement of low structures. There were greenhouses and what I took to be potting sheds, tool-sheds, and the like. A group of three men waited outside one of the sheds. Two had armed themselves with gardening forks and stood ready to repel whatever was inside. Their attitude suggested it might be a bear, wolf, or other dangerous animal. The older man was evidently a gardener, a stocky fellow of middle years, face darkened by the wind and sun, his clothes all weathered and stained to an earthy brown. His fellow, looking rather less composed, was a boy of fourteen or so, probably one of the indoor servants—a footman rather than a kitchen helper, judging from his outfit.

There was no mistaking the identity of the leader. I had never met our employer, but the man in a tweed jacket with a shotgun tucked under one arm could only be Mr Randolph Stafford. He was tall but stout, making his height less apparent. His build suggested a placid, cheerful individual. That day, he was profoundly troubled.

I knew little about Mr Stafford, having felt it wise not to ask questions, but I gathered he came from a good family and had increased his fortune by trading in the city. A touch of grey about the temples suggested he might be in his early fifties, but he was ageing well.

"Thank heaven you're here," he said with feeling. "I thought you'd never come."

"What's the situation, sir?" asked Skinner.

Stafford ran a hand through his hair before answering. "It's the under-gardener, Pierce." The tremor in his voice signified a man trapped in a nightmare. "He has lost his mind. We've cornered him in the shed here, but he won't come out."

"And you require some assistance in restraining your under-gardener," said Skinner as though we were dealing with no more than an escaped rabbit. "I take it he is displaying signs of violence?"

"Some signs." Stafford raised the shotgun almost apologetically. It was a fine weapon with filigree work around the barrel. "This is just birdshot to keep him back if he turns dangerous. Just to be safe."

"I see." Skinner turned to the younger of the servants. "You run along now, sonny, and fetch us a couple of pairs of thick gloves—one medium-sized, the other the biggest you've got—at least two lengths of decent rope, and a canvas bag big enough to put over his head. Quick as you can, now! We'll see he doesn't get out while you're gone."

The boy stood his fork against a greenhouse and hurried off while Skinner and I removed our jackets.

"What would you like us to do with him once he's restrained?" asked Skinner.

"We'll clear a room for him in the house until I can arrange a suitable asylum." Stafford was less agitated by then. A confident NCO can calm the jitters of the most anxious officer. "Pierce is a good man when he's in his right mind."

"He ain't in his right mind now," said the old gardener.

"Is he frothing at the mouth?" I asked.

"No, no," said Stafford. "It's not rabies."

"Still, you can't be too careful," said Skinner. "I'm not planning on letting him bite me. I do know also that madmen can be extremely strong; it can take six men to hold one down... but the five of us will be enough since we have Mr Stubbs here."

The small greenhouse next to the potting shed looked new and was empty except for a single tray of earth from which green shoots poked upwards. Perhaps the gardeners had been interrupted while working on it.

The young footman came back, arms full with the items Skinner had requested.

"Rope's not the problem. Getting him tied up's the problem," grumbled the old gardener.

"Just hit him over the head with a spade," said the footman, looking at me.

"Head injuries are dangerous," I said. "And if he's fighting mad, then it's a fine balance between stunning him and crushing his skull. Pinioning him would be greatly preferable, in my view."

"Yes, absolutely," said Stafford.

"As the professional, I look to you in the matter of close-quarter tactics, Mr Stubbs," Skinner said. "How do you recommend we proceed with this here operation?"

The four of them looked at me expectantly. Any protest that the current situation was nothing like boxing would be in vain. I'd been involved in numerous ructions in my capacity as a doorkeeper, though, and had also had occasion to apprehend individuals with regard to discussing their financial obligations. Though hardly a professional, I had a wide informal experience in this field. My lack of formal training made me feel like a pretender, but I tried to emulate Skinner's air of confidence.

"You stand over there," I said to the boy. "Your job is opening the door but not until I give the signal. Skinner, you position yourself here next to me, ready for him. And sir, if you can stand well back, you can provide covering fire if need be."

My plan was for Skinner and me to burst in, seize the man, and drag him out into the open. The head gardener would be ready with the ropes and canvas so we could make him fast as soon as possible while Stafford covered us with the shotgun. He and the boy would provide extra support in the struggle as needed.

"Nice day for it," said Skinner, matter-of-factly unfolding the blade of his pocketknife and tucking it in his waistband at the small of his back. I flexed my fingers; the gloves were a tight fit, but they were stout leather. If being bitten was a hazard—and it might well be in a struggle with a madman—then my hands would be well protected. The gloves also provided padding, so I could hit him with decent force without so much fear of damaging either him or me.

There was a slight smile about Skinner's face. His cheerful demeanour was not, I saw, because he was careless of danger but because he welcomed it.

For my part, I was inclined to caution. I rolled my shoulders and dropped to my haunches a few times, loosening up. Then I moved into a fighting stance.

A bumblebee rose from a bright tulip, which swayed to and fro. It was indeed a nice day for it.

"Everyone ready?" I asked. "Open the door—now!"

The footman threw back the door and leaped well clear, revealing a shadowy interior. Wooden shelving filled both sides of the shed, leaving a narrow space between. A man crouched low against the far wall. He was a small fellow in a white shirt and dark trousers. The way he was hunched suggested a hunted animal.

"Come on out, Pierce," Stafford ordered. "There's a sensible fellow. Nobody means you any harm."

We waited several seconds, but the fugitive did not move. I nodded to Skinner and stepped forward. As I did so, Pierce bolted. He moved faster than I would have thought possible, but not so fast that I could not shoot out a hand to grab his shoulder as he passed.

"Stop there, you," I said.

An ashen face looked up into mine. His complexion was completely bloodless. I might have been looking at a corpse except for those wild, terrified eyes. The whites were visible all the way around, and his pupils were oddly colourless. For a moment, Pierce did not resist, then he pulled away suddenly. The awkwardness of the heavy gloves betrayed me, and Pierce twisted and slipped out of my hands before I could get a proper grip on him.

As Pierce passed, Skinner tried to lay hands on him but was thrown off. None of the others was ready to grab him, and Pierce had broken through the cordon. The barrel of Stafford's shotgun veered wildly, first high and then low as if to shoot the fleeing man in the legs; luckily he did not risk a shot. Pierce dashed down the path with the rest of us in pursuit. I was in the lead, cursing myself for letting him go and determined that he would not escape again. He was faster than most.

Pierce took a sharp turn past a shed and then another towards a door in the garden wall, but he veered away when he saw it was padlocked. The whole place had been secured.

I was gaining on Pierce when he ducked through a row of tall, bushy trees—the leylandii variety if I am not mistaken. I plunged through after him into a small, paved court with a fountain, but there was no sign of which way he had gone. There were several possible exits.

Skinner was with me two seconds later. "Let's just go very easy here. The grounds are secure, so we don't need to be hasty. Let's spread ourselves out a bit but stay so we can see each other. Anyone sees or hears anything, shout out."

"Understood," I said to show support, and the others murmured assent.

"Let's try the far corner," said Stafford, and we set out abreast with Skinner and me slightly in the lead.

As we passed the house, I saw pale faces looking down at us from the upper windows. Stafford's wife and daughter peered out of one while at another window stood a little group of servants, anxious spectators of our little drama, hands clutched in front of them. Skinner gave the audience a half-ironic salute when Stafford's back was turned.

"That little housemaid is a cracker," Skinner said in a low voice, and the footman shot him a black look. Matters can get intense with people working in the same house together, day in and day out.

Pigeons started into the air as we rounded a neatly trimmed hedge. On the other side was a lawn as smooth as a billiard table. The birds' wings clattered as they cleared the garden wall. Stafford gripped his gun and scanned left and right.

"There he is!" shouted the old gardener.

A woodshed leaned against the wall, and our quarry was trying to get onto the roof by climbing the pile of chopped firewood stacked by it. The footman rushed in, ignoring Skinner's shout to stay back and, in two leaps, was up by the madman, grappling with him.

"Bloody young fool," Skinner muttered, and we dashed after him.

A second later, the footman was thrown down and sprawled at full length of the ground.

Pierce took an axe from the woodpile and was waving it at us, two-handed. "I didn't do anything!" he shouted. "Leave me be!"

"Calm down, Pierce," Stafford said. "You're sick."

Skinner and I advanced on him. Pierce was at the top of the woodpile, perhaps four feet off the ground. If I came forward, I could grab his ankles, but that would mean taking a blow to the head from the axe.

"Don't be an idiot, Pierce," said Skinner, sidling closer. "Your master here has a shotgun. You make a nice big target for him up there. Do the clever thing and come down."

"I won't do it!" he wailed and swung the axe at Skinner, who nimbly stepped back out of the way.

I judged the moment and stepped in to grab the axe on the follow-through, catching the haft close to the head with both hands. Instead of letting go, Pierce held on. I gave a smart tug, and he overbalanced and fell off his perch. Skinner and I were on top of him in a trice, rolling him face downwards and forcing his arms behind his back. Pierce struggled, but madman or not, he was no match for the two of us. The scuffle concluded with me holding Pierce down, one knee on his back. Pierce stopped struggling when he realised the futility of his situation.

"Give me that cord!" Skinner ordered. The old gardener was helping the fallen boy, but Skinner found the rope, and we made the prisoner fast. My partner's skill with knots was impressive. I hauled Pierce to his feet.

"There you are, sir," said Skinner. "All nice and tidy."

Stafford was distracted. The piles of wood for chopping up included some old timber frames, part of a greenhouse or similar, with long, rusty nails protruding. The servant boy had put his hand down when he landed so that one of the nails went clear through his palm and out the other side. The old gardener helped pull him free, but the boy whimpered in pain, and blood was spurting from his hand as from a garden hose. The old gardener staunched it with a neckerchief, and Stafford ordered him to take the boy to a doctor while the rest of us went to the house.

We delivered the prisoner to a cellar and lashed him to a chair. He was subdued by then, mumbling words to himself I could not hear. It sounded like an incantation, repeated over and over. Once he was safely secured, two of the female servants tended to him.

"I'm sorry your man injured himself," said Skinner. "I tried to stop him, but –young men get carried away."

"Not your fault," said Stafford complacently. "He had some previous history with Pierce."

Our patron was well satisfied with the outcome. He was a well-meaning sort. His authority had been re-established, and everything was in its place, the errant under-gardener stowed safely away where his ravings would not disturb the peace.

Freshly raked gravel crunched underfoot as we walked back to the open gates. Someone would need to rake it over again to erase our footprints and preserve the look. I asked Skinner if he could make out what Pierce had been mumbling.

"It was that old saying," said Skinner. "'First a man takes a drink, then the drink takes a drink, then the drink takes the man.'"

"He didn't look drunk to me; he looked ill."

Skinner shrugged. His view was that it was better not to ask questions, and he did not seem curious. But I had reminded him of something, and he passed me a handful of coins. "I touched his Lordship for a gratuity. Expenses, wear and tear caused by the operation, and such like."

We passed through the gates, and Skinner paused to light up a cigarette.

"It's a bad business," I said. "I hope the footman recovers from that wound—he could lose his hand if there's an infection. I don't like to profit from it."

"I certainly don't intend to lose by it," said Skinner.

Chapter Three

At the Sign of the Knyght's Head

While I finished writing up the report, Skinner kept reading and rereading the letter he had taken from the rooming house. "Maybe whoever wrote this letter could tell us what a beetle is—and what this is all about."

"There's no name and no return address on it."

"Maybe there isn't, and maybe there is," Skinner said, scrutinising it with a magnifying glass. "She did not write her address on this one, but she did write it on the sheet of notepaper above. And we might just be able to get an impression."

Skinner took a soft pencil and moved it quickly across the paper, up and down, shading in one corner. He triumphantly slid it over to me. Sure enough, the ghostly negative image of writing could be made out.

"It's the Knyght's Head in Norwood New Town," I said. "If the woman who wrote this lives there, I suppose she must be the landlady."

"That's a low establishment," said Skinner, whose knowledge of local pubs was encyclopaedic. "We'd better pay her a visit this evening before our assignation. I'll stop by the Hollybush first and see if anyone can put a name to her."

"Assignation, did you say? What assignation?"

"His Nibs wants to meet us in Norwood Park after dark." Skinner raised his hands. "Don't ask me why. Orders is orders."

Norwood New Town had always had a reputation as a tough neighbourhood. The six streets of back-to-back terraced houses had been intended for the workmen brought in to construct the

Crystal Palace back in the last century. To protect the established residents, a high wall surrounded the New Town, preventing the inmates from mingling too freely with their betters.

The wall told every man inside the New Town that he was a rough fellow. Some of them were pleased to live up to that reputation and embellish it. The wall stayed up and had two gates, one of which was usually shut. The police did not go in there without a purpose, and on those occasions when they did show up, they moved in force, stifling any possible disturbance.

Arthur Renville had contacts and business dealings with everyone in the Norwood area and beyond, but he said the New Town was a blank space on the map. In those few streets, it was every man for himself, and the essential trust for joint enterprises like Arthur's was lacking. Poverty had corroded the machinery of cooperation. Arthur said the New Town was cannibal territory, not quite in a literal sense but metaphorically: men feasted on each other when they got the chance.

Skinner insisted that we should dress for our visit to New Town in our shabbiest clothes. I wore an old cap instead of my usual bowler. There was no sense in drawing attention.

I had never visited any pub in the New Town before, but the place offered few surprises beyond being spelled "Knyght's Head" on the faded sign, a peculiar olde-worlde affectation for a modern establishment. It was a shabby, raw place that, unlike more affluent drinking locations, did not make the pretence of being a gilded palace or a gentleman's club. Or even a halfway comfortable lounge. Everything in the pub was functional, and there was a notable lack of breakable decorations such as mirrors or large windows. Even the ashtrays were tin. It was simply a place where men came to drink beer, together or alone.

Hard lives had sculpted the regulars at the Knights Head. They were shorter than most, stunted by lack of food in early life but made broad and hard by long years of physical labour. Their faces had a windswept, blasted look from exposure to all weathers. They were not the "honest English yeomen" that our politicians romanticised but men with dirt under their nails and mouths full of the foulest abuse who couldn't even talk about the weather without spitting and swearing. They expected nothing out of life and carried with them a sullen pride that, despite all of the world's attempts to grind, hammer, and wear them down, they were still stubbornly there.

They were the most fundamental of labouring classes: the unskilled workmen. They were despised, but they'd built London brick by brick, mended the roads, dug up streets, laid water and sewage mains, and torn up everything to make room for bigger and newer buildings. To them, anyone who did not work with his hands was soft, contemptible, and overprivileged. They gave skilled workmen grudging respect. Shopkeepers like those in my family were viewed with suspicion as idlers loafing behind a counter who overcharged workingmen and deprived them of money for beer.

As individuals, they might be good men and a sight more honest than their social betters on the average. There was no mealy-mouthed manoeuvring or fast-talking with these types, and in their circles, your word really was your bond. A debt was never forgotten, and you could almost always get them to pay up eventually.

But when you got a few of them together and under the influence of drink, it was another story. An ugly side came out then, especially when there were outsiders to confront.

Skinner breezed in, nodding to an imaginary acquaintance and sidling up to the bar as though he was a regular. He ignored the sullen, silent gazes that followed us from all sides. I slunk behind him, as much as someone of my build could slink.

There were two people conversing behind the bar—an older man in a stained shirt, unshaven, with the blurry look of a habitual drinker, and a young woman in a dress that left her shoulders and much of her chest bare. The older man had barely registered our presence before the woman was leaning towards us attentively, and he went back to staring into the distance.

"Two pints for a couple of thirsty men, Elsie my angel," Skinner said to the barmaid.

"Do I know you?" she asked, taking down two glasses. Her hair was blond, and a quantity of gold jewellery glittered on her arms and chest, making her look like a Christmas decoration. This would be the letter writer. Skinner had established her name by enquiries elsewhere.

Skinner clutched his chest. "Such cruel, cruel beauty. Your indifference pierces my heart. Have you forgotten me already?"

"Yes," she said, well used to the way of men with barmaids.

Skinner passed the first pint my way. The head was not promising, and the beer was watery and sour.

"As a matter of fact, I visited a mutual friend this morning," said Skinner casually. "In West Norwood."

The barmaid gave Skinner a sharp look before turning her attention back to the handpump. "I'm not playing guessing games."

"I don't know if I should mention her name," he said. "We're not police. I don't want to get anybody into trouble."

"You can mention any name you like."

"Mabel Brown," Skinner said softly.

"Never heard of her," said the barmaid without a flicker. "That's eightpence."

Skinner took a long, slow drink, watching her all the while, making no move to pay. "Never heard of her?" he said, putting his glass down. He felt in his pocket and took out the envelope. "Never heard of her?"

She just had time to read the address and recognise her own writing before he replaced it in his pocket.

"Nobody else knows about you and her," he said. "It's just between us for now. All we want is some information."

"Talk to her, then."

"Mabel is nowhere to be found," he said, raising his eyebrows. "Just fancy that."

"I don't know nothing."

"That's good. Knowing nothing is very good. Saves a lot of trouble, knowing nothing." He took another slow drink.

The barmaid, Elsie, looked on, waiting for him to continue. That envelope clearly bothered her.

"We're not going to make any trouble, I assure you," Skinner went on, putting a shilling on the bar. "We're going to drink up and leave quietly. If, that is, you say the magic word that'll make us disappear and never come back."

"What word?"

"A word about a beetle."

"I don't know nothing about a beetle."

"A minute ago you didn't know anything about Mabel Brown," Skinner reminded her. "Maybe we'll wait another minute."

"I've never even seen it. Why don't you leave me alone?"

Skinner nodded again as though she had told him something interesting. "Why is it so valuable?"

"That letter is private correspondence. Give it me." She held out her hand.

"If you tell me what makes the beetle so valuable."

"I don't know anything about it. It's not a proper beetle anyway. It's Greek thing."

"So perhaps you can tell us something..." he coaxed.

Elsie stepped back and rang the bell over the bar, the one they ring for last orders. The whole pub fell silent.

"Free drinks to everyone who helps throw these two bastards out," Elsie announced, pointing at the two of us in case there should be any doubt as to who she meant.

The scene was like one of those famous cartoons by H. M. Bateman—"The Man Who Lit His Cigar Before the Loyal Toast" or "The Shareholder Who Dared To Criticise The Chairman's Report." In those cartoons, the whole room goggled with various degrees of comically exaggerated horror and outrage at the man in the middle who had committed some terrible social gaffe all unawares.

At that second, with all the attention focused on me, I knew exactly how it felt to be one of Bateman's socially inept men. Elsie was the pub's darling, and we had offended her. I could not have caused more upset if I had gone around and spat into every pint of beer individually.

The difference between us and an H. M. Bateman cartoon was that we had not just made a blunder that would result in uproar and hurt feelings. These men were as hard as any in South London, and defending the honour of their Elsie would require inflicting physical pain.

It seemed to me then that the pub rose as one man. In most situations where a fight was in prospect, my brain would start working in double-quick time, but for one moment, it just jammed up, overwhelmed by the sheer scale of the opposition.

I was paralysed, but Skinner had already seen and planned and sprung into action. "Get 'em, Harry," he said, skimming his cap like a discus. It flew at tabletop height, upsetting glasses so the owners stepped back from a torrent of spilled beer. The tactic might win two seconds or so. If we had been near the exit with a clear way out, it might have helped, but a solid wall of outraged workmen blocked our way to the door.

Someone grabbed my right arm, and reflexes took over. I gave him a quick jab to the floating ribs with my left, and he doubled over. A second man approached, and I hit him high in the chest with a blow that was more of a shove. He was upright, not crouched, and the impulse of the blow so far above his centre of gravity sent him toppling backwards.

I had a clear advantage in height, being a good head taller than any of them and with a correspondingly greater reach. If they could get close enough to wrestle me, it would be over. However strong you were, you couldn't win when there was a man holding each of your arms and others are hitting and kicking you. But nobody could wrestle me without passing my fists.

I was seized from behind. Rather than trying to break free, I jerked my right arm back smartly. I judged the height pretty accurately, and my elbow connected solidly enough with a face. As my assailant let go, I whipped round and followed up with two quick-fire jabs.

The men were pushing forward, shoving the tables and benches aside to get at me, and I delivered some long punches. Hitting a man bare-knuckled calls for judgment. It helped if you had the reach and could avoid striking the hard bones of the jaw and breaking your fingers. When I hit the first man, his dentures flew out and onto the floor, an occurrence that might have made me laugh in other circumstances.

Beside me was a flurry of movement; Skinner broke free of two men trying to hold him and vaulted cleanly over the bar. He shoved the surprised Elsie aside and went through the doorway. Then I was busy knocking them back, manoeuvring as best I could with my back to the bar.

I was surrounded by a semicircle of perhaps twelve of them, two deep. My assailants were getting up almost as fast as I was knocking them down, but it was all one-sided. None of them had managed to land a blow, and the assault slowed. Their initial enthusiasm had been quenched, and the mob was hesitating. Those who had been knocked down were not keen for another dose of the same.

They seemed to have lost all individuality, and every one of them had the same face, compounded of sullen rage and bloodlust. I thought they were going to rush me in a body, and I struggled to think how I might defend myself when they did. Instead, one of them shouted out:

"Belts!"

Belting was a time-honoured means of punishment round those parts. It was usually doled out to gang members who failed to toe the line, or to other transgressors. The victim had to shield his face from flying belt buckles and had no chance of getting back at his tormentors. It usually ended with him on the floor getting a kicking until they decided he'd had enough.

The first belt whipped at me, moving slow enough for me to dodge it. I stooped and grabbed a stool as another cracked painfully over my shoulder. Then there was such a volley of belt buckles whipping at me that all I could do was try to defend myself with the stool and, with my free hand, grab any belt I could catch hold of and haul on it to disarm an attacker or pull him over.

That was quite a game. It was a fairer game than it seemed, though. The coordination between my attackers was poor, and if they were strong, they were not all sober, and at least one of them kept tangling the others when he missed, hitting them in the face. With a bit of sidling left and right and judicious ducking, I reduced the rate at which the blows landed, but all I could do was play for time.

A piercing whistle cut through the tumult—the double blast of a police whistle, deafening in the close confines of the pub.

My attackers froze, some of them dropping their belts in an attempt to look less guilty. Past them, Skinner beckoned me from the pub doorway, the silver whistle between his lips.

I did not need any encouragement. It was now or never, and I charged forward, clobbering two men aside with the stool, fending off belts left and right, and shoulder barging the only man directly in my way. I was out of the door in four bounding paces. Then I was running up the street with Skinner beside me.

We broke records for the hundred-yard dash going up the street. I could hear footsteps behind us and I was convinced the pack would catch up, but between the narrowness of the doorway and the fact that they had to hold their trousers up, we had the edge in speed.

We hurtled back up to the entrance to the New Town, where two policemen were looking down towards us, their attention no doubt attracted by the sound of the whistle—and by the mob appearing behind us. They let us through then closed the iron gates behind us and shot the bolt with a clang. The footsteps behind faltered and died away in moments.

"What's all this, then?" demanded the constable.

"Slight misunderstanding. In the Knyght's Head," said Skinner, out of breath. "Caused offence. No harm done."

The constable looked us up and down, giving us time to feel uncomfortable. "Public brawling. Causing a disturbance. A charge of affray might be brought, in fact, there being two of you involved. What do you have to say for yourselves?"

"I'm very sorry for the disturbance, and I assure you nothing was further from my intention. It was, as I say, a very unfortunate misunderstanding involving a lady."

"I see," said the constable, reaching ponderously for his notebook and pencil and turning to me. "Stubbs the boxer, isn't it? Been using your famous fists tonight, have you? Are you supposed to be Skinner's bodyguard?"

"I acted exclusively in self-defence when we were set upon by a mob in consequence of my associate's conversation being taken amiss by a young lady, Officer."

The constable permitted himself a small smile. "At the Knyght's Head? That was no lady, Stubbs—that was Elsie Granger! As pretty a she-devil as you'll find this side of the river. What did you want with her?"

"We were visiting in a professional capacity," said Skinner. "Unfortunately, our enquiries were not welcome." Then he leaned closer and said something in a voice too low for me to catch.

"I hope you've learned your lesson," said the constable, replacing his notebook. "You two won't be allowed through this gate again. There's enough trouble in New Town without you stirring people up. Understand?"

"Yes, sir," said Skinner.

The constable tapped his nose. "Keep it clean, Skinner. You too, Stubbs. We'll be keeping an eye on you. Off with you, now."

Chapter Four

Counting the Stars

Fish and chips were a great restorative, and Skinner insisted in paying for what he called "land and sea" for the two of us. He made a point of demanding an extra-large battered cod for me, a thing that I never did for myself. I didn't mind paying for an extra saveloy to make up the protein. Skinner ordered it served with the newspaper wrapping open so we could pick at our food as we walked down the street.

"Sharpens the old appetite, doesn't it?" he said cheerfully through a mouthful of fried potatoes.

"I thought we were dead there."

"I never felt so alive in my life," he said. "Danger is a better relish than brown sauce. Besides, they wouldn't do any worse to you than break a rib or three."

"Have you ever had a broken rib? It's not pleasant." I munched a morsel of cod. The batter was crispy and sharp with the tang of vinegar, and the flesh was soft and succulent. Skinner was right; imminent death did sharpen a person's pleasure in the good things in life.

"Strange, alien creatures, women. She was playing along nicely when she just snapped," mused Skinner, looking into the evening sky. "Impossible to understand 'em."

I could hardly comment on that, but something was still puzzling me. "It's not a proper beetle. It's a Greek thing," I said, repeating Elsie's words. "What does that mean?"

"Greek to me," said Skinner, chuckling at his own wit.

"What did you say to the constable?"

"I dropped the name of our employer. Sometimes it works."

Our employment has always been veiled in ambiguity. On the one hand, it was suggested that we had some sort of sanctioned, semi-official status, but everything had to be kept a secret. Skinner said it was like being spies but in our own country. He had no curiosity about the matter. It was enough for him that we were paid well.

We chatted idly as we ate, until Skinner looked up at the big clock outside the Foresters' Hall and said we should to be on our way. "Just agree with everything he says. Otherwise, keep your mouth shut, and you won't go far wrong."

Skinner led me along Central Hill to Norwood Park, which normally offered a majestic view of the City of London to the north, with the dome of St Paul's and all the church spires visible on a clear day. The view was not so impressive with dusk falling and the stars beginning to peep out. Away from the streetlights, the shadows deepened into full darkness—not like country darkness or the dark of a coal cellar, but the city kind of dark, where shapes were outlined against an ever-present background glow.

"Hey there, you two." A tall, stout figure waved his cane at us. "Over here."

"Good evening, sir," said Skinner.

"A fine evening, Skinner, Stubbs." He was looking up into the sky. "Just as I hoped, the stars are out. Come this way. I want to explain some things to you."

Even in the dark, Skinner's look said *I told you so* as clear as day.

A good officer never needed to explain. He'd give orders, his men would obey, and the whole thing would function like clockwork. But some officers felt a need to explain the whys and the wherefores and were not happy unless you agreed with them. It betrayed a lack of confidence and bred a lack of belief. The men laughed at them and walked all over them.

The only thing worse was an officer who wanted to be your friend.

Stafford led us into shadows, where the slope was steeper, and surprised me by lying down on his back and indicating for us to do likewise. "Now, look up. Give your eyes a minute to adjust, and you'll see more stars. Do you see them?"

"Yes, indeed I do, sir," said Skinner. "Is that the Plough over there?"

"Ursa Major. Indeed it is. Stubbs, do you see the stars? Do you know how many stars there are?"

"Yes, sir. No, sir, I can't say that I do."

"Well, keep looking."

We lay there in the quiet and the dark for a minute, and sure enough, I could see more stars than before, the fainter ones appearing out of the velvet night between the brighter stars.

"On a good night in a properly dark place, you can see far more than this." Stafford was almost apologetic; this was something that mattered to him. "Ptolemy made the first star catalogue in the second century AD, with more than a thousand stars in it. Flamsteed listed more than two thousand—of course, they were using telescopes by then. When I was at college, my professor told me there were fifty thousand stars. Since the turn of century, though, with these new telescopes, we can resolve much fainter stars, and now we talk in millions. Millions of stars… can you imagine that?"

I scanned from horizon to horizon and tried to think what a million stars would look like. Even that many would not quite fill the heavens, but they would look like the sparkles on a sunny sea, all packed close together.

"But then," he said, "along came Professor Hubble, who has just discovered the universe!"

"Pardon me, sir?" said Skinner.

"Edwin Hubble. An American but a remarkable astronomer. They have the most astonishing telescope in California, a hundred incher. And with it, Hubble discovered that the Andromeda Nebula, among others, was not part of the Milky Way."

"Did they think it was?" asked Skinner.

"We thought everything was part of the Milky Way," Stafford said. "But Hubble showed that it was a separate galaxy in its own right. And that there were many, many others like it."

"So what we thought was the whole universe was only a

small part of it," I said once the silence had stretched on.

"Exactly so. Now you have to consider just how vast the universe is that Hubble discovered."

"I've no idea," said Skinner, failing to sound amazed but adding "sir."

"Let me put it in terms that you can more easily understand. Suppose you had always lived in a closet six feet by three, and that was your world."

"A closet, sir?" asked Skinner.

"Six feet by three," Stafford repeated. "And as far as you knew, that was the total extent of Britain. Then one day, the door was opened, and you were let out into a mansion with halls and corridors and chambers, a thousand times more space than you had ever known. That was Ptolemy, and the ancients who realised that there were many worlds. You know the story about Alexander the Great sitting down and weeping because there were no more worlds to conquer?"

"I've heard that," I said.

"It's a canard, a lie. When Anaxarchus told him that there were many worlds, Alexander wept because he had failed to even conquer one. It's in Plutarch."

"Quite so, sir," said Skinner.

"But that was the ancients. What Hubble has done is like opening wide the doors of the mansion so you can see beyond. All around you is the vast metropolis with many more houses bigger than the one that you've seen. And beyond that, the rolling fields of the Home Counties, the cities of the Midlands, the Lake District, the vast expanse of the Yorkshire Moors, on and on to the Highlands of Scotland and then endless islands, and the smallest of the islands is infinitely bigger than what you took for Britain. It staggers the imagination."

"It's a dizzying prospect," I agreed, having given up the contemplation of it early on.

"There are other countries besides Britain," said Skinner.

"Exactly," said Stafford. "Hubble has expanded the bounds of the universe to an almost unthinkable degree. But who is to say that's the end of it? With every era, we find a bigger and bigger universe. Even if you ever did finish exploring the British

Isles, you would then find an even greater world beyond."

"I see exactly what you mean, sir. The universe certainly is very big," said Skinner.

"Big enough to contain marvels and wonders," said Stafford. "And we are arrogant enough to believe that this little speck of dirt, this little broom closet we live in, is the pinnacle of creation?"

Neither Skinner nor I felt equal to a reply. Fortunately, none was expected.

The stars did look quite lovely; I had never taken time to look at them before, twinkling away up there. Most of them were plain blue-white, but others were yellowish, and one winked almost scarlet like a blood ruby. And just as Stafford had said, as my eyes adjusted, I could see more and more of them. Some of the fainter ones looked smeared out—galaxies or nebulae perhaps, archipelagos of millions of stars.

"Once, when I was a boy, I got lost in the woods. The sun had moved out of sight, and the darkness was growing… and I saw something wonderful, something that changed my life. It was a burning bush—a bramble bush with a cold, prismatic light playing over and through it without consuming it. Of course, I knew my Bible, and I was terrified. I ran away as fast as I could… if only I had known about Blake's vision, his tree of angels with their 'bright angelic wings bespangling every bough like stars.'"

I made a mental note to find out more about William Blake, though I suspected he was tangential at best.

"The next day, I set out to find it. When I got there, the brambles were gone, crumbled away to nothingness, leaving only fine grey dust. All that was left was one withered stalk with a couple of leaves and a single berry."

That made my scalp prickle. "Palingenesis," I whispered.

"Something very like it," said Stafford.

"Palingenesis is an alchemical trick whereby a plant, burned to ashes and crushed to powder, can be restored to life," I told Skinner. "But only for a time, then it returns to powder."

"I knew that fire was something extraordinary like the Pentecostal tongues of flame or the Holy Spirit itself," Stafford went on. "For years, I forgot about it completely. Then just a few months ago, I saw it again—in the heavens."

"How was that, sir?" Skinner enquired.

"I was looking for a periodic body with my telescope, one that has been hinted at by the Arabs but never confirmed by European astronomers. Such bodies appear only rarely in our skies in their eccentric orbits. When I saw it, I knew it at once. It was a nebular glory unlike anything in the catalogues, a living, moving thing in space. A hundred years ago, they might have called it an angelic host. I tried to capture it on a photographic plate, but all I could get were dull blurs. The glass could not hold it. The next night, it was gone. None of the astronomers I corresponded with saw it—or admitted to seeing it—but I knew that it must mean something. It woke something in me."

"That would be when you employed me," said Skinner.

"And you have been invaluable," said Stafford. "I found there were connections with other mysteries and strange sidelights on points referred to by Paracelsus—much of it thanks to you, Skinner. That was when I put out an advertisement, one that would only be understood by those who know, and I started to get replies."

"I'm glad to be of service."

"Such a shame about the Theosophical Circle," Stafford said to me. "Yeats, he was on the trail—him and some of the others in the Golden Dawn. If only he hadn't gone to the Irish Free State! He knew about the 'silver apples of the moon...'"

W. B. Yeats, the noted poet, had associations with the theosophists, including the Theosophical Circle, which had been torn apart in the Roslyn D'Onston business. He was also a member of the Golden Dawn, a society dedicated to the study of magic. But the reference to silver apples left me baffled.

"I'm not familiar with that one, sir," I said.

"It doesn't matter. It was just a thought. I say, does either of you know Eliot's *The Waste Land*?"

"T. S. Eliot's poetry is a little too modern for me, sir," I said.

"I'm rambling," he said suddenly. "I'm sorry. I must sound like an absolute raving lunatic sometimes! My nerves are shot after today's business. I don't know what I would have done without you. But I'm trying to get to the point. My advertisements had some positive results. Most of the replies were obvious frauds, but a couple... I was too eager. I sent money, and my correspondent wanted more and still more before she would send me the sample. This was via a Post Office Box number."

"Luckily, though," said Skinner picking up the story, "the identity of a box owner could be established with some persistence and greasing of palms, which I duly undertook. And that was what led us to Miss Mabel Brown. The late Miss Mabel Brown."

"Dreadful what happened to her," said Stafford offhandedly. "But we must find the sample she had and, most importantly, where it came from."

"We'll find it," said Skinner. "Though it would be helpful if you could supply some particulars of what this thing or substance is. Or how it relates to beetles."

"I don't know anything about beetles," said Stafford, and I could hear the frown in his voice. "But I guarantee that you will know when you find it. You will not mistake the Holy Grail! If only I can find it, ah, then..."

Stafford seemed to lapse into reverie in the dark.

After a decent interval, Skinner asked, "Will that be all, sir?"

"Yes, yes, that's all," Stafford said, rising stiffly to his feet and brushing off grass. "I hope you've found this useful. I do so want you to understand how much it means, this search."

"We do understand, sir," said Skinner, counterfeiting enthusiasm. "You can rely on us to do our duty."

"Yes, sir," I added.

"Very good." Stafford turned to go. "You have your instructions. Carry on."

"What was the significance of all that?" I asked in an undertone when Stafford was a safe distance away.

"Your guess is as good as mine, Harry. Just nod and agree with them as though it makes perfect sense—that's what I do." He laughed.

"What does he mean with all that stuff about stars?"

"You mean, what does it have to do with the price of fish? Nothing that I can see. Anyway, you've met him now. Puts things in a new light, doesn't it?"

I had made certain assumptions about the man I was working for—that he would be a wise and learned man with a secret fund of knowledge. I had not expected that he would be a lone eccentric who talked fervently about God and stars and poetry and the Holy Grail.

"And what was that about Paracelsus?" I asked. I knew him as the hero of Browning's epic and, more importantly, the alchemist who had first discovered palingenesis.

"Oh, him," said Skinner as though the sixteenth-century physician was someone he had met in the pub. "He wrote about stars and their effect on health, and minerals in spring waters and suchlike. I had to acquire some of his manuscripts for our patron. By hook and by crook."

"Was that difficult?"

Skinner chuckled at the recollection. "It is when the books don't even exist! There are some very eccentric gentlemen in the antiquarian book business who are worse than him by a long chalk. And mugs like you and me running around finding things for them. Still, it's no worse than the war. The money is better, and there's less mud and shelling." And though he would never admit to it, Skinner loved the adventure as much as I did. "We've time for another drink before closing time, and I expect you could use one right now."

"Not for me." I knew that Skinner would be on the brandy and would get morose and start talking about the war. He was a man whose drinking went through stages. For the first drink or two, he would be garrulous, cheerful, and making a joke out of everything. Then he would mellow and enter a quieter phase, letting others do the talking. Then towards the end, he would get melancholy, and all his old grievances would come out. Skinner had never freed himself of the war, and he took his dark recollections out and polished them like service medals.

While most men got more boisterous with drink, Skinner was normally cheerful when sober but was overcome by a slough of misery rising from some inner depths when alcohol dissolved the barrier holding it back. I preferred my drinking companions a bit more cheersome. Besides, it was getting late.

Chapter Five

An Unexpected Visitor

I had been in the office for some time, writing out my notes and making a list of many questions and a few possible leads, when Skinner finally showed up. He looked seedy. Evidently, the night had not refreshed him.

"Morning, Harry. I've such a head on me today... you're bright and early as always."

"I've been trying to make some sense of it all," I said.

"Give up on that for starters," he said, slumping in his chair. "Let's just do what we're told. I'm happy to say that two cups of Horniman's finest brew should be coming through shortly, and then I'll start functioning. I'm just sorry I didn't put in an order for a stiff brandy with it."

"Soda water would do you more good," I said. "And my trainer swore by raw eggs for a hangover."

Skinner made a face, but at that moment, I heard a commotion and raised female voices in the outer office. We both looked round as the door opened, and in marched Elsie Granger.

"Good morning, gentlemen. Aren't you going to offer a lady a seat?"

I sprang up to give her my chair, there being only two in the room. She looked smaller than the previous night, wearing a modest lavender dress with long sleeves and a high neck, but still formidable. She carefully removed her cloche hat and placed it on the desk.

"Well, this is a pleasant surprise," said Skinner, covering his confusion. "And you seemed almost unfriendly last night."

I was wondering how she could have found us, though in hindsight I suppose we were quite a distinctive pair. Perhaps one of her cohorts had found out our identities from the police constable, or maybe someone had recognised me from the ring.

"She's gone," said Elsie, fixing him with a hard look. "I went to Mabel's rooming house. She's disappeared with just the clothes on her back and one suitcase. I want to know what you know about it. And I want my letter back."

"We're not responsible," I said. "We just wanted to talk to her."

Elsie's eyes traversed the office, from Skinner to me and back. "Insurance business, is it? Insuring what, might I ask?"

"I believe we mentioned our interest in the *beetle*," said Skinner, with emphasis on the last word. "And that's all about it."

"All I know is that she has this thing, and she was trying to sell it," Elsie shot back. "She was scared of the people who wanted it—I expect she meant you two. She asked me about getting some lads for protection while she did the deal."

Everything that Elsie said we could have gathered from the letter, but she told us as though she was conveying new information. "Now, you tell me what happened to her."

"Somebody killed her," said Skinner.

"Killed?"

"I'm afraid so."

Elsie swore under her breath the way you might if you stubbed a toe. But she did not seem surprised.

"We don't know who. The only clue we have is this." Skinner brandished Elsie's letter to Mabel Brown, keeping it out of her reach. "Maybe we should give it to the police."

"You wouldn't dare."

I snatched the letter out of Skinner's hand. Hung-over as he was, he was not quick enough to offer any resistance. I handed it to Elsie Granger.

"We're investigators, not blackmailers, Miss Granger," I said. "And we'd greatly appreciate your assistance. We need to locate this 'beetle.' We haven't even got a good description of it at present, but I'm sure it will lead us to her killer."

I strove to ignore Skinner's angry glare.

"Well, now," she said, slipping the letter into her bag and tucking it protectively under her arm. "Thank you kindly, Mr—Stubbs, is it? I honestly don't know anything; I never even saw it. It's not a *beetle* beetle—I know that. It's a Greek thing. And she said it was ever so valuable."

"I don't suppose she mentioned how she came by it?" Skinner asked.

"Not likely!" She practically laughed in his face. "I barely talked to her. I knew Mabel years ago at school. She went off to the West End to be an actress." From Elsie's tone, *actress* was a cut or two below *barmaid*. "I never even heard from her until a week ago, when she comes round out of the blue, asking for my help. I never asked where she got it… maybe an admirer gave it to her. Or she stole it from him, more like."

"That's not much to go on," said Skinner.

"It's all you're getting," she retorted. "And if there are any official investigations, you'll see my name doesn't come up, won't you?" She held Skinner's gaze for a moment. "I know how to find you now."

"Thank you very much for helping us, Miss Granger," I said.

"Don't mention it," she said, standing up and taking her hat. "I'll see meself out."

She went with a confident step, and shut the door behind her with some force.

"That's a woman as would rattle your bedroom windows," said Skinner half-admiringly.

I was thinking more about how little interest Elsie Granger had taken in the death of her friend. She had barely asked after Mabel Brown. Her attention was stuck on the fabulously valuable beetle.

"I'm sorry I acted out of turn with that letter."

"'Out of turn' doesn't cover it! You seem to forget that I'm in charge around here." Skinner was not given to being officious, but he was sensitive to being shown up in front of others.

"It was a spur-of -the-moment thing. I thought relinquishing the letter would—"

"Oh, leave off," he said, softening. "It doesn't matter. I reckon we got everything we were likely to get out of her anyway." He raised his fists, about as menacing as a boisterous kitten. "But if you ever flout my authority again, Stubbs, I'll beat you a pulp with my own two hands!"

I could not help laughing, and the atmosphere was restored. Skinner's mood was further improved when one of the office girls came through with a tray bearing two steaming mugs.

"My angel!" he said. She fled, giggling through her hands.

"And now we're pretty certain," said Skinner, between blowing on his tea, "that the body in the suitcase was Mabel Brown and that someone killed her and took the body away—and most probably our elusive beetle at the same time. So who could that someone be?"

"Logically, it must needs be one of the other occupants of the rooming house. Or else they would have to be uncommonly quiet and sneaky. Sneak in, murder Mabel Brown and put her body in the case, sneak out before we come, sneak in again, and then sneak out with the suitcase, all without being seen."

"Makes more sense for it to be one of the residents. We need a woman on the inside to find out. See if that suitcase, and the beetle, are still on the premises." I could see Skinner's mind working. "The landlady has decided Mabel Brown has gone, so she'll advertise that room for let. All we need to do is get our girl to take it."

"Our girl. How about Elsie Granger?"

"No! As if they'd let a barmaid in a respectable place like that anyway. What we need is a decent girl who can let the room and make some discreet enquiries about who's who. Anyone spring to mind?"

"It's no use asking me," I said. "You're the one with all the acquaintance among the fairer sex."

"Lucky in love," he said. He appeared to be going through a mental filing system of likely women, smiling with fond if vague recollection. "Not so many respectable ones, though."

I also doubted how many of them he was still on good terms with. Skinner's many amours, by his own admission, were brief flings. They floated like bubbles, sometimes for as long as a week, before bursting. Mostly these liaisons dissolved with the dawn, and next day, he did not always remember her name.

That might put the burden on me. I had never before considered my lack of female acquaintances. Apart from my sister-in-law and a few sisters of friends, I was not on first-name terms with any women. Debt collection, the pub, and the boxing gym were my world, not circles in which women were admitted.

"We could ask one of the women here, one that you get on with," I said, nodding towards the door and the chinaware-packing concern beyond.

Skinner chewed his moustache a moment. "No, not a casual acquaintance. We need someone we can trust."

"Come to think of it, there might be one woman I know. She doesn't exactly owe me a favour, but—"

"Ask her then," said Skinner. "We can pay, if that'll help. All she needs to do is find out who in that house knew Mabel Brown, who talked to her—and who might have that suitcase in her room. "

"And there's something else," I said, pulling out the slip of paper I had found as a bookmark in *The Prairie Bride.*

"D'you think those notes mean anything? Janitor? Archivist?"

"Not the notes—look at the paper," I said. Skinner looked at it, starting to read the recipe for duck ragout before I drew his attention to the edges of the paper. "It's been cut out of a book. She didn't tear out the whole page from *Mrs Beeton*; she sliced out a rectangular section in the middle. And I was thinking, why would she do that? And then I thought, maybe she cut out hundreds of pages—"

"And hollowed the book out to make a secret compartment," Skinner concluded. "We never searched the books. So that's where it was hidden."

"And just maybe it still is."

"That's a long, long shot, Bombardier. But we'd be fools to pass up the chance. This woman of yours—how soon can you talk to her?"

Chapter Six: The Spy

I am not by any means a habitué of tearooms, and my visits are invariably on family occasions when the gang of us gather for a celebration with fancy cakes and sweet biscuits. I am always aware of the risk of damage to the fragile crockery, and I move carefully so as not to upset the entire table. Much as I enjoy fairy cakes, the experience is never entirely comfortable even when I'm surrounded by my family.

How much more it played on my nerves to be sitting at a table on my own, feeling eyes on me from all sides, waiting for a lady. *Who's he waiting for?* The thoughts were so loud I could almost hear them.

At five in the afternoon, I was the only male in the place, apart from one or two of the children. The waitresses moved about quickly, negotiating the swinging doors to the kitchen with ease, carrying trays with arrangements of cups and teapots and little plates, and dodging past each other with admirable footwork, especially considering the shoes they had to wear.

"I am so sorry I'm late," said Sally, putting her bag down by the table. "There was such a scrum at the bus stop I had to let two buses go before I could get on."

Sally was a very different woman to the thin, pale creature of a few months past. She had filled out a little, and her complexion was quite rosy. Her hair seemed different though I could not say how. She sat up straighter too, and looked around her with something like authority instead of timidity.

"Two teas and two fruit scones," she told a passing waitress, who mouthed *Yes, Miss* without stopping. "And aren't you the fine one—you look like a business tycoon."

I was wearing my good suit for the occasion, the one handmade by my Chinese tailor, as I did not want to appear scruffy. Sally's outfit was a plain brown dress but not unfashionable as far as I could tell.

"I must say," I started out, "how very much I appreciate your helping me. It was a great deal to ask, and at such short notice—"

"Give over. It got me away from the nuns."

Sally had been living at the Virgo Fidelis convent and doing menial work to pay for her keep, a position that had been secured for her by my mentor, Arthur Renville. Sally had suffered a nervous breakdown, which had necessitated the move. The reason for that breakdown was an encounter with what I can only call a grotesque undead being. That had been at the very start of the Roslyn D'Onston affair. I had interviewed her on the matter with Mr Yang, and she had provided some valuable clues that led to the resolution of the case.

I dropped by on a subsequent occasion to let her know the final outcome of that case. I had hoped that knowing it was over would ease her nightmares, and Sally had been fulsomely grateful to hear that the dead would henceforward stay dead. After that, she had recovered greatly and had reached the stage of looking for new employment and lodgings by the time I contacted her.

"I've got a job in the pickle factory," she said. "So it all fits together nicely. All part of His plan, as the nuns would say."

"You got a job just like that?" I asked, amazed. There were men at the gym who had been looking for work for months.

"There's plenty of jobs going for women round here. They ain't very well paid, though."

"I'll make sure you're recompensed for the assistance you're rendering us," I said.

"Don't you fret about that. You just put in a good word for me with Mr Renville. Once I'm back on my feet, I mean to get my little boy back—he's with my sister and her husband." She looked down at the table. "If Mr Renville can speak for me, it would make a world of difference with my brother-in-law."

That was new information to me. All I had known about

Sally was that she worked on the streets under the protection of a man called Collins, who'd since departed for parts unknown. I had no idea she had a child—and presumably a husband somewhere. I looked reflexively to see if she was wearing a ring, but of course she was not, and she smiled at my confusion.

"He fell in the canal, drunk. Drowned."

"Who?"

"My husband. I've been a widow three years. It was always going to happen; he drank that much. And after that—but you don't want to hear about my troubles. You want to know what's going on in that rooming house." She leaned closer. "And I've got it for you, all cut and dried. Seven women, and one murder suspect who stands out like a sore thumb."

Sally had only been in the house for one day. I closed my gaping mouth just as the waitress arrived and efficiently delivered doilies, teapot, cups, saucers, cutlery, sugar, milk, two plates with scones, a butter dish, and a miniature porcelain jam pot before taking off again.

"That's some fast work," I said. "You must be Sherlock Holmes. But nobody mentioned murder."

She brushed my assertion away with a gesture. "Mrs Berry, the landlady, is an old chatterbox. That woman would explode if she had to keep a secret for fifteen minutes." Sally poured an experimental dribble of tea to check the colour then filled two cups and added milk. "The other girls in the place are one typist, two secretaries, one dressmaker's assistant, and one American writer. Plus, Mrs Berry herself, and me working in the factory and smelling of pickles, for which I do apologise if it puts you off your tea."

"An American writer?"

"A lady writer. Miss De Vere. The others had been there for years, but your Miss Brown had only been there three months, and this writer lady for two weeks. And guess who strikes up a friendship with Miss Brown the minute she comes through the door?"

"The American lady, De Vere?"

"She says she's writing a book about modern life in England." Sally raised her eyebrows. "That's what she says.

She goes around *interviewing* everyone. She even wanted to interview me, but I said no, thank you, I don't want to be in any book." Sally's eyes narrowed. "She's got money, that one. Silk stockings on Monday afternoon. And has a car to pick her up, if you please. And she's always off to the West End to *meet someone*—commodores and company directors and people. She says."

"She may be suspicious," I said, pausing with cup halfway to my lips. "But not necessarily the only suspect."

"The others are as plain as anything. All chitchat about Valentino and shingling and which boy will take them to the dance on Saturday. I know their sort." She leaned forward again, elbows on the table. "Miss De Vere was the only one who ever talked to Mabel Brown. And she was the last one to see her the night before."

"You didn't ask her—"

"I'm not daft," Sally said. "She doesn't suspect me. If I was of a romantic turn—which I'm not—I'd say Miss De Vere was an international jewel thief. She has that air about her."

"She sounds worth investigating."

"Hmm. You be careful about investigating her. She'd have you for breakfast."

I decided to ignore that slur. "Did you find anything out about Miss Brown?"

"I was just getting to that," said Sally, putting her untouched scone on my plate. "Here, you have mine—you need feeding up. Mabel Brown is a woman of mystery, sort of. Very evasive about where she came from and what she did and everything. The one thing that Mrs Berry did know was that Mabel Brown worked at the museum. Mrs Berry insists on an employer's reference before she lets a room out, you see. And when she disappeared, Mrs Berry checked with the museum, and they hadn't seen her either."

"The museum" could only mean the Horniman Museum. It commanded the borders of Dulwich like a medieval castle.

"Now, that is most interesting," I said, spreading a thick layer of jam over a thick layer of butter.

"Isn't it? Perhaps Mabel's an international jewel thief too. If they have jewels at the museum."

"What sort of reference does Miss De Vere have?"

"She wears furs and a diamond bracelet and an alligator-skin handbag," said Sally, sniffing. "And she pays in advance. That's her reference. As though money has anything to do with respectability. Quite the opposite, in my experience."

"I think you should leave that house now. You've done an excellent job, and I don't want you in any unnecessary danger."

"It is murder—Mabel Brown's dead, isn't she?"

I spent longer chewing and swallowing than necessary. "I'm not free to comment on that. But hypothetically speaking, if something happened to her and if Miss De Vere had something to do with it and if Miss De Vere suspects that you have an interest in the case, then you might be in some danger. There's no reason for you to go back there. We could send someone to collect your things."

"Oh, and speaking of collecting things, that reminds me—they've already collected her things. Mabel Brown's. A second-hand shop took them, including that *Mrs Beeton* book you were asking about. I didn't have a chance to get to them."

"That's worth knowing," I said. "There's no reason for you to stay, then."

"If I just leave without telling her, poor Mrs Berry will think there's something wrong with her house. I'll stay there a few more days until I can find an excuse, but I'll leave off my investigations. I'll let you know if Miss De Vere gets up to anything."

"I don't want you poking around or doing anything that might alert her." I was thinking of the suitcase full of blackened bones.

"You may worry about me, but I worry about you, Harry Stubbs. You came through last time, but then, Mr Yang was with you, and he was a gentleman even if he was Chinese. Trustworthy. Your friend Skinner, I don't call him reliable, especially not when it comes to women." She stopped suddenly. "Those two over there are talking about us." She indicated with a jerk of her head where two older women conspired over an arrangement of yellow-and-pink cakes. "They probably think we're illicit lovers having a tryst."

"Why illicit?"

"Because it always is illicit lovers, isn't it?"

"They could think I'm a private detective you've hired to find some missing diamonds."

"Then why would you be whispering? No, you're a detective who's been following my husband, and you're spilling the beans about his illicit love affair with his secretary."

"Your mind runs to forbidden love," I said.

"I expect it's the sort of books I read," she said, putting down her teacup. "But I promise I'll be very careful if you'll do the same."

"I promise, Sally, that I'll be careful."

Not that being careful would be enough, as I was shortly to discover.

Chapter Seven

J. P. G. Higgs

There is a hierarchy in the business of disposing of unwanted goods. At the pinnacle are those who are pleased to call themselves antique dealers, who handle the rare and valuable items. On the very bottom rung are the rag-and-bone men who take any and all rubbish for the value of its material—bones to be rendered down for glue, rags to turn into paper, a thousand types of scrap metal, and wood for furnaces. In between these two poles is a world of second-hand traders and pawnshops, all with subtly different gradations of affluence and honesty.

The business of J. P. G. Higgs, Esq. lay very much towards the lower end of the scale. His premises occupied a small warehouse with a sagging roof, located on a street off the brickyard. As we approached, the sky was clouding over, and it looked like we were in for rain. I tried not to see the gathering clouds as an omen.

The front door was wedged open. Skinner dropped his cigarette stub and ground it into the pavement, allowing two men carrying a trunk between them to go ahead. We followed them in, where they were met by a middle-aged woman with gold pince-nez.

The room was like a church-hall jumble sale with trestle tables, some of them bare and some piled with all sorts of goods. The men carried the trunk to an empty table and threw it open. The woman drew on a pair of mismatched dirty kidskin gloves and placed a mask over her mouth and nose before rifling through the contents, which seemed to be mostly women's clothes. She picked through them with the rapid, efficient gestures of a professional scavenger, quickly evaluating the contents.

I began to discern an order in the layout of the room. The tables in the middle were unsorted items recently arrived, while round the outside, everything of value was collected by type. One table held nothing but umbrellas of all shapes and sizes; another was in two halves, with coloured medicine bottles on one side and spectacles on the other. There was a sad little pile of dolls and teddy bears in one corner. I looked in vain for where books were stored.

The woman passed over a handful of coins; the men touched their caps and filed out.

"Good morning, madam. Mrs Higgs, I presume," said Skinner, removing his hat. "Mr Skinner and Mr Stubbs for Mr Higgs, if you please."

"Good morning," she said, pulling the mask off her face. "It's the germs, you know. You can't be too careful."

"No indeed," said Skinner. "Mrs Higgs, we were looking to purchase a certain item that was accidentally included in a lot sold from Norbury Avenue. An item that was not, in fact, the property of the vendor."

"Is that right?" Then, turning her head, she said, "John! Two gents here for you."

In the quiet that followed, we could hear the pattering of rain on the wooden roof above.

A door opened into a sort of cabin suspended above one end of the hall. An elderly man in a dusty velvet jacket looked down on us with appraising eyes then made his way down the wooden stairs. His progress was purposeful but unhurried.

"Says there was something in a lot from Norbury Avenue," she called to him.

Higgs was short, almost gnomelike, with a few grey hairs plastered across his pate and eyes that glittered with cunning.

"Mr Stubbs," he said, raising a hand in greeting but not offering to shake. "Formerly collecting for Latham and Rowe, I think. Now with a new employer?"

"Stubbs and Skinner of Lantern Insurance, at your service,"

said Skinner, proffering a business card with a slight bow.

Higgs accepted the card and read it carefully. "Norbury Road, you say?" he said thoughtfully. "Have we had anything from there recently? I don't recall."

"Wouldn't like to say," added his wife, taking her cue and moving to stand beside her husband.

"A woman moved out owing rent, and the landlady disposed of the contents of her room," said Skinner. "I have it on good authority that your van called by to pick up the effects."

Husband and wife exchanged a look. They were old hands at this game.

"Well, we must have done, then," said Higgs. "If you say so."

"There were some books," said Skinner. "Including a copy of Mrs Beeton's cookbook."

"A very popular volume." Higgs's knowing smile grew a little. "We've probably got a dozen of them in stock if you want one."

"This was a very special copy. It was hollowed out with a secret compartment inside."

"I'm sure I'd remember something like that," said Higgs. "You haven't seen a hollowed-out book recently, have you, Edith?"

"I don't know as how I have."

That was very much as expected. They would certainly have found whatever was in the book, and simply by being there, we showed that it was valuable, if that was not obvious already. Our presence also suggested that it might be stolen property. Higgs had no need to talk to us. He could simply show us the door, if he felt like it, and see if he could find a buyer, which made Skinner's next move inevitable.

"Pity," said Skinner, gazing at a gold sovereign that had appeared in his palm then flipping it casually into the air with his thumb. "We would have paid a good bit for it."

Skinner always said that a sovereign had far more attractive power than any amount of silver coinage and more even than folding money with a nominally higher value. Gold had a primeval hold over the hearts of the acquisitive; it called out to them in a way that no other currency could.

Higgs tore his gaze away from the spinning coin with difficulty. "Now I think of it, there was a little thing in a copy of that very book you just mentioned. You just wait here a minute."

He went back up the stairs to the office, fishing out a bunch of keys on a chain from his pocket as he did so.

"Filthy weather," remarked Mrs Higgs, glancing upwards towards the roof, which was starting to resound with the hammering of rain.

"Maybe we can get you to throw in a couple of used umbrellas as part of the deal," said Skinner.

A minute passed, during which the metallic clanking sounds of a cash box being opened came from upstairs. Higgs reappeared, holding a silver cylinder, which I first took for a saltcellar. When he held it in his palm in front of us, I saw it more resembled a miniature vacuum flask.

"That might be it," said Skinner.

"Five pounds, sold as seen," said Higgs slyly. "Take it or leave it, as you please."

"I believe you paid ten shillings for Miss Brown's effects all told."

"I'm entitled to a fair profit," Higgs said, nettled. "You think it's easy work, picking through this filthy trash, day in, day out, everyone trying to cheat you? When some weeping widow brings me her dead husband's mildewed old coats, I can't turn her away with nothing, can I? When people get turned out on to the streets and want me to take their worthless belongings, old Higgs always pays up. I have to pay for everyone's rubbish—it's expected. Nobody is ever bothered about me making a return. I've got to make my living somehow."

Higgs's anger was entirely manufactured. He must have trotted out the same speech so many times that he had worn the shine off the argument.

"You have no idea," Mrs Higgs chipped in, supporting her husband. "The hours we spend, the filth we have to go through. Fleas and lice and nits and all sorts of crawling vermin. I wash my hands in bleach, I do. There's things that people hide away because they don't dare throw them out. The things in tin trunks and old boxes that end up here—they'd turn your hair grey."

"Is that so?" asked Skinner.

"I could tell you stories," she said. "When you die, relatives don't dare go through your belongings. We have to do it."

"We're entitled if we do find the odd coin or bit of jewellery," said Higgs.

"That's all very fine and worthy of you, but we don't have unlimited funds at our disposal," said Skinner. This was largely a bargaining ploy; Stafford would probably have paid a fortune, but we did not want to alert Higgs to just how valuable the item was.

"I'm not asking for unlimited funds, Mr Skinner; I'm asking five pounds." Higgs held up the silver cylinder. "It's yours if you want it. But that's my last and final offer."

I sensed a ruse, and I thought I could see through it. Skinner was probably well ahead of me, but I spoke up anyway. "Five pounds. And that would be including the original contents."

"I can't say what's in it," snapped Higgs. "Like everything here, sold as seen."

A tremendous boom and crash from above us shook the whole building. For a moment, I thought the entire structure was going to come crashing down about our heads. The blast sounded like a bomb. Skinner and I involuntarily ducked. There were further sounds of falling glass and debris from the upper level.

"Lightning," said Mrs Higgs.

"The cash box!" shouted her husband, racing up the stairs twice as fast as he had come down them. He opened the door, and great clouds of smoke billowed out; tongues of flame whipped up behind them. Higgs threw himself into the room beyond, ignoring the fire.

"He shouldn't have done that," said Skinner.

I started up the stairs, but before I reached the top, Higgs emerged from the smoke, holding a weighty iron box in his arms. "I've got it," he said, coughing and almost doubling over.

I went to help him with the box, but Higgs's eyes narrowed, and he snapped at me angrily. "Get away, you! I can carry it myself. I'm perfectly capable." His words were cut off as he stifled another fit of coughing.

The strong box was a type I had seen before. During the night, it would be securely bolted to the wall or floor, and in the daytime, it functioned as a cash box with a double lock. What made this box unusual was the fresh mark stretching down one side.

It is difficult to describe exactly what happened next.

Things could not really have occurred the way I remember them, but in my memory, everything went blue-white for a moment. It was as though I was standing inside an enormous photographer's flashbulb. I was completely dumbfounded by the light before the shockwave hit. It felt like being punched in both ears at once. I had the presence of mind to hold on to the handrail and prevent myself from falling backwards.

The reverberation continued while bright, vertical blobs danced before my eyes, and it took a second for me to recognise the shrill sound beneath it as a woman screaming. Then someone took my arm and urged me downstairs.

"Move yourself, Harry!" Skinner was bellowing in my ear. He sounded a long way off. "Jump to it, quick!"

The world was still full of white fog wherever I looked, but I had recovered enough of my senses to follow as Skinner pulled me along and through a doorway into the rain outside.

"Stay here!"

I sensed him recede again, and a second later, there was more shouting. My vision was clearing, and I could make out Skinner as he dragged Mrs Higgs bodily out through the door.

"Take one arm!" Skinner ordered. "Get her across the road."

As Skinner was struggling with her, I found it more opportune to take both her wrists in my hand and more or less lift her off the ground to go to the other side of the road. We were not halfway there when our three shadows jumped out ahead of us, and there was a concussion from behind as lightning struck a third time. The thunder boomed and rolled around us, and it seemed to bring down so much rain it was like standing under a waterfall.

"Jesus Christ," muttered Skinner.

By that time, Mrs Higgs was not offering any resistance. I

passed her to Skinner and dashed back across the road. There was still a bright shape on the left side of my vision when I blinked, but I could see well enough to get through the door.

Any thoughts that I might save Higgs, and perhaps even win his gratitude, evaporated as soon as I saw him. He had been thrown from the stairs. He had landed on a table piled with clothes, which had collapsed beneath him. The soft landing had not saved him. I could tell from one look that he was quite dead. Lightning was not invariably fatal, but when it passed through the body, as it had in this case, death was instantaneous. Mr Higgs's burns did not appear extensive, but the bolt had passed from his back through his chest. His heart and lungs must have exploded from the electrical force of it. Higgs's arms were locked in place as though he was still holding on to the strong box, but they were clasped around empty air.

The box itself lay in the far corner by the pile of dolls. It had been struck three times by lightning but showed little damage except that the area around the lock had a blackened look to it. It was not rusty or melted, but the iron had been eaten away, enlarging the keyhole into a ragged gash, which exhaled a twist of brown smoke. The lightning had sought out the box and wormed inside it, blasting and melting and vaporising the contents. The inside of the box would be a melted puddle of gold and silver.

As I approached, I felt the brush of static electricity through my hair. Whatever was drawing the lightning was still active though not as vigorous as it had been a few minutes earlier. I backed hurriedly away. A thin layer of silver-grey smoke had settled and was disappearing between the floorboards like viscous liquid. Stroke by stroke, the beetle was being disintegrated and finding its way to the ground. I did not know what to make of it.

Several neighbours had appeared under their umbrellas and were confusedly questioning Skinner and the inert Mrs Higgs in spite of the pouring rain. Another bolt of lightning flashed out, and we all saw the windows illuminated with blue-white light as it struck inside. The reverberations of the thunder hammered down upon us. It went on for far longer than normal thunder.

The lightning was the signal for us to all move inside to the next building, which was a furniture-restoration concern. Four or five workers left their places to crowd round as we entered.

"Higgs is a goner," I told Skinner.

"I know. I saw him. No luck with the box? Didn't think so. Look, you'd better slope off and let me talk to the law. We'll RV and debrief back in the office later."

"Of course—I can trust you."

"Harry," he said seriously. "Don't ever trust me. Just act in your own interest—it's what I do."

Chapter Eight

First Encounters

I have ceased to attend Upper Norwood Library. I would not wish to be recognised there, following the unfortunate incident during the Roslyn D'Onston affair. The library at West Norwood, which is just as convenient, is my new haunt whenever I need to draw on the well of reference works. It is not as grand, but it does have the busts of great writers of the ages looking down from the façade. I like those wise, solemn faces. They're like ancient kings who have hewn out this grand kingdom from words and invited us all to share in it.

For my part, my respect for books runs deeper now than it ever did, but Skinner does not believe there is anything useful to be gained from libraries. He says he had a bellyful of training manuals and books of regulations in the army, and that was enough reading to last him a lifetime.

After our misadventure with Higgs, Skinner was pleased enough to see me go off to the library for an hour. He could doze undisturbed in his chair in the drowsy afternoon warmth without even the pretence of staying awake.

At first, I was reasonably successful. I looked up what I could find on lightning and how it could be drawn to a particular object. The encyclopaedia, my usual starting point, had little to say beyond lighting rods, but I came across an old book of lightning lore that looked more promising. It described thunderstones—flint or other stones shaped like arrowheads—which had been found at the site of a lightning strike. According to some traditions, these thunderstones had the power to draw lightning as well as being able to repel it, though modern science had nothing to say on the matter.

A thunderstone, or some similarly compact object, might have been contained in the silver flask, which would have blocked its powers. When Higgs had taken it out, the stone had quickly drawn lightning, with the catastrophic results we had witnessed.

Without wishing to, I saw again Higgs's body, wracked by the lightning stroke. It was quite different from Mabel Brown's charred skeleton. Whatever had reduced her to that state had been far more thorough than lightning but surely must have been connected to the thunderstone.

And in any case, how did one get from something shaped like an arrowhead to a beetle? There were electric eels and other electrified fish, but as far as I could discover, nothing like an electric beetle. The Americans talked about "lightning bugs," another name for fireflies, which were in fact a form of winged beetle, but they were not actually electrified in any way. Perhaps closer were the bombardier beetles that ejected an explosive charge… but this was taking me wide of the point if the "beetle" was not a beetle in the literal sense.

I could not find the right section in the library by wandering around, so I addressed myself to the filing system. This was series of index cards on yard-long drawers that slid out of the wall.

I was on my knees, going through one drawer of cards, when someone said, "May I help you?"

My interlocutor was a senior member of the library staff, a man with half-moon glasses and a neatly trimmed beard. Neither his expression nor his tone was friendly.

I could hear Skinner's voice somewhere in the back of my head saying I should tell the librarian to sling his hook and leave me in peace. Skinner could never understand why I did not impose more on people, given my natural gifts in that direction. But Skinner's ways were not mine. I could not so easily ignore the man's rightful authority.

"Um, I-I'm not sure," I stammered.

"Do you know what you're about with the card index?" His

tone indicated that I did not, that I was sabotaging his well-ordered system, that in my clumsiness, I would mix up the cards or lose them.

"I'm still finding my way."

"Perhaps you could tell me what you're looking for. The Dewey Decimal System is a finely tuned instrument for extracting information. It is not, however, suitable for casual browsing by the uninitiated." He gave a tight little smile. "Unless you have an unwarranted faith in the probability of pulling needles out of haystacks."

I put the cards back, very carefully, and stood up. "I'm not really sure where to start. It's to do with beetles…"

"That would be under 'science, biology, zoology, other invertebrates,'" he said crisply. "Second aisle on the left—595, I believe."

"Thank you very much."

The librarian's brusque manner was not actual hostility but more like impatience. His was an orderly brain surrounded by the chaos of a disorderly world. He had the whole universe of human knowledge at his fingertips and was forced to spend his talents on enquiries from subscribers who knew only that the book they wanted was a small green one.

"What is a beetle when it is not a beetle?" I asked.

"Are you looking for the answer to a riddle?"

"In a manner of speaking…"

"Jokes and riddles are classed under humour. That would be 810, I believe. Though it might be under 'children's.'" Again, that small reflexive smile. He liked knocking back answers like tennis balls—rapidly and with a bit of spin.

"It's more complicated than that," I said.

"I am here to help."

His tone was far from warm, but he did seem receptive. It was almost like a challenge. On the basis that I had nothing to lose, I recited a bowdlerised account of the hunt for the beetle, shorn of most of the details but playing up my role as a collector of debts. By the time I had finished, the librarian seemed absorbed in the problem.

"Have you a valid library card?"

"I do," I said, producing it for his inspection like a passport at the border of a new country.

"Very good. Well then, Mr Stubbs," he said, reading my name from the card, "what you would be looking for would be a homonym, or more likely a homophone, of the word *beetle*. A homonym being another use of the same word—such as *beetle* employed as a verb—and a homophone being a word that sounds the same but is spelled differently. The latter seems more likely, with the additional information that it has a Greek root."

I nodded dumbly and followed him to the dictionary section, where he selected a thick volume as big as a church Bible, opened it skilfully, and ran his finger down the page.

"It would have to be a noun," he said. "There is a homonym, in fact, from the Middle English. A beetle is a type of mallet with a large wooden head used to drive wedges. What do you think?"

"I had better write this down," I said, getting out my notebook.

"By extension, beetle is also a type of hammering machine used to flatten cloth. Also, a shelf or ledge." He looked up. "That seems much less likely. On the homonym side, it might refer to the seed of the betel palm, known as a betel nut, which is popularly chewed in parts of India, Ceylon, and China. It is used to stave off the effects of hunger and dyes the chewer's mouth red."

"That's also possible."

"Do you do cross-word puzzles?" he asked. "I'm rather addicted to them myself."

Skinner sometimes did the cross-word while I was doing paperwork or writing up my notes, and he called out for assistance with some of the clues. Between the two of us, we could fill in most of a puzzle. I suspected my new benefactor filled them in rather more rapidly on his own.

"I'm a beginner," I said.

"You can generally tell when the answer is right for a cryptic clue, and this is the same sort of thing. Frankly, I'm not convinced that the answer is either a medieval mallet or an Asian nut. Neither of those quite fits, and certainly not with the supposed Greek etymology."

"What's the answer, then?"

He spent another minute checking through the dictionary, perusing other possible spellings such as "beatel" and "beital." At length, he closed the book. But he did it with the determined air of one who will not be beaten.

"It seems," he said, "that we are going to need a bigger dictionary."

"Is there a bigger one than that?"

"Of course. The complete OED is comprehensive. They have one at Dulwich. That's twenty volumes. I'll send a query over there for you now."

"I couldn't really—"

"But I could. And I shall. Please drop round here tomorrow morning, and I think we will have the answer for you, Mr Stubbs."

"I'm very much obliged to you, Mr…?"

"Hoade," he said. "Assistant Head Librarian Hoade."

I was still thinking about my encounter with Mr Hoade that evening when I repaired to the gym. A man who could reach down into the archives and pluck out knowledge of the ages as easily as picking out a couple of pork chops was a useful ally. I was already beginning to compile a list of things that I might ask him, but I put all those thoughts away as soon as I reached the changing room. I would need all my mental focus. I had been invited that evening specially to spar with a promising young boxer from Sydenham, a heavyweight called Sammy Gold. He was reaching the point where nobody else there was able to handle him. His trainer felt he was ready to move up a size.

Sparring was an essential stage in learning how to box. There was a world of difference between punching a bag and fighting, and sparring provided an intermediate step between the two. In sparring, you wore protective headgear, and punches were limited to body shots only, but it still had the most important elements of a real bout and sifted the fighters from the flops.

All the regulars at the gym, along with a whole gang of visitors, were gathered to watch. I nodded to Skinner, who was always at his ease in a sporting environment though perhaps disappointed that he could not bet on the outcome.

This was Sammy's first trial at a higher level, and everyone wanted to see if he was the stuff champions were made of. He looked nervous as a racehorse and kept adjusting his mouthguard and brushing his hair back with his gloved hands. He looked at me as if trying to see my weaknesses by X-ray, while I made my own estimates of his reach and agility.

Gold was better than I thought—fast, disciplined, and strong. He was better, in fact, than anyone I had fought for a while, and that put me right on my mettle. It was only sparring, but I had no intention of losing to a beginner, not even one as skilled and determined as Gold.

In terms of strength and reach, we were pretty well matched, and he could take a punch. The crowd was quiet to begin with, but as soon as they saw it was a real match, they warmed up. The gym rang with shouts of encouragement and advice, and two-thirds of them were cheering on the newcomer. If he could beat me, it would be an upset of epic proportions, and he was strong enough to do it.

When it came to tactics, though, Gold was a slow learner. He did not vary his moves through the whole fight, while I was constantly adjusting and trying new ways to work round him. His footwork was routine, and by the third round, he was dangerously predictable. If an opponent kept dodging the same way, sooner or later he would dodge into my left fist.

I came to respect Gold, though. At the start, he was neither intimidated nor overconfident, and when I began to get the upper hand, he did not fade but kept coming back with good, solid punches and well-drilled combinations. My armour, composed of slabs of muscle, was in good condition, or those blows might have ruptured some internal organs. Or at any rate, that was what it felt like. The boy could punch.

It was a warm evening, and we were both sheathed in sweat well before the end. Unlike many youngsters, Gold did not run out of steam but kept going full bore. If I had relaxed my concentration for an instant, I would have paid dearly for it. But I did not relax my concentration; Harry Stubbs was still a match for any beginner.

The bout carried on at a furious pace through every round, right through to the final bell. It was no easy match, but the referee duly declared me the winner and held up my gloved hand. I made Gold raise his too, and that got a cheer. He was not my equal yet, but he had years ahead of him to learn. Certainly, he was better than I had been at his age, and who could say how far he would go?

"That's your baptism of fire," I said.

"You weren't pulling your punches, were you?" He did not quite sound as though he believed it.

"Did it feel like I was?"

Sammy Gold grinned, and I remembered the exhilaration of my own early days in the ring. The next morning he would be aching, but that night, he was on top of the world.

"You're a good fighter. I'll give you some tips later," I said.

I shook hands with Gold's trainer.

"The raw material's all there," he said confidentially. "I've just got to keep him away from wine, women, and song for the next few years. Easier said than done with some women."

When I emerged from the changing room, a boy pushed through the well-wishers to tug my sleeve and tell me that Mr Skinner needed to see me at once. I found him sitting in one corner at a folding card table. Opposite him was a blond lady in an outfit of filmy, clinging material. She was dressed more stylishly than I would have expected for one of Skinner's companions, and by any conventional standards, she was beautiful.

I wondered at first if she was one of that breed of upper-class women who were excited by the sight of blood. They would come to see you after a fight, eyes shining, and paw at your biceps while their male companions—short, fat, balding—watched with neutral expressions and burning eyes. But her manner was more that of a teacher who had witnessed a playground scrap than a boxing enthusiast, and she seemed bored rather than excited.

"Harry," said Skinner, winking at me, "allow me to introduce Miss Estelle De Vere from the United States."

"Pleased to meet you." She inclined her head slightly. I had never heard a real American accent before. It was something like Irish but milder.

Up close, her looks were even more striking. Her figure, her complexion, her features were flawless. I was uncomfortably aware of my misshapen nose and mutilated ear.

"Miss De Vere tells me she is writing about British sporting life," said Skinner. "As your agent, I said you won't mind being interviewed."

Miss De Vere fitted a cigarette into an ivory holder. Skinner was ready with a struck match as soon as she raised it to her coral-pink lips.

"We don't get many women in here," I said.

"I go where the story takes me," she said, blowing smoke and speaking as though she could hardly be bothered to make the effort. I was to find she was more used to getting answers than providing them. "I guess that's something you two gentlemen… can understand."

The bag on her lap matched her dress. One hand rested on it as though ready to draw a weapon. For some reason, I immediately wondered if she was one of those women who carried a bottle of vitriol around with them for self-defence. She was not quite so relaxed as she wished to appear.

"Is this interview to be mainly about boxing?" Skinner asked.

"Only if you can't think of anything more important to talk about." She was cool and amused, verging on rudeness. I suppose you might say she was provocative. Like Elsie Granger, Miss De Vere had the determination to seek us out in our own haunts. But the two women were otherwise quite unalike. Elsie was raw and brash; Miss De Vere was smooth and feline. Where Elsie was brassy, Estelle was refined, spun gold.

We did not know how much she knew about our investigations, and Sally had not provided much information. You could waste a lot of time dancing about at the start of a fight and tire yourself out, so I decided to take the direct approach.

"There is the matter of Miss Mabel Brown," I said. "Maybe you could shed some light on that."

I do believe she blinked, but she replied with the same easy drawl. "She played with fire. You know what happens... when you play with fire?"

"You get burned," I said.

"Ex-actly. Just like that unfortunate Mr Higgs. I guess you had a pretty close shave there." She looked up at me from under her lowered lashes. "I do hope you know what you're doing."

"We're masters of improvisation," said Skinner. "But we can always use a few pointers if you'd like to clue us in."

"Well, now. You fellows are in a dangerous line of business. Some of us think Pandora's box should stay shut."

"I'm afraid you might have to elaborate on that," I said.

"Greek myth. The gods give this woman a box with all the troubles of the world in it. Her husband is warned not to open it, but of course, curiosity gets the better of her. Pandora opens the box and..."

She made butterflies with her hands; her frosted pink fingernails matched her lips. My own hands on the table were hairy paws, meaty and clumsy.

"They had to blame a woman, of course. Truth is, it's always men who open the box. Always letting out all kinds of trouble. Men like..." She looked upwards to let us know she was referring to Stafford.

"What about Mabel Brown?" I asked.

"She got caught up in the middle. She died by... *misadventure.* I tidied up the mess afterwards."

"You said 'us,'" I said. "Who are you?"

"Yes, I did say 'us.'" The blue eyes were amused by my attempts at interrogation. "An association of like-minded people. Between *us,* we have a certain amount of influence. And we'd like to prevent... more serious misadventures."

Usually, Skinner asked the questions, but he seemed content just to sit by Miss De Vere, a lizard basking in the warmth of the sun.

"The sort of misadventure that might be brought about by gentleman scholars," I said.

"Those old forbidden books are forbidden for a reason," she said. "But some people just don't get the message. They find these loose threads in the fabric of reality, and they just can't leave them alone. Someone has to stop them unravelling it."

I thought of the Shackleton case and also the Theosophical Circle and its too-great enthusiasm for the study of palingenesis. Both had been instances of Pandora's boxes being opened, with disastrous results for those concerned. And also, of course, I thought of our patron and how his interest had indirectly caused the deaths of Mabel Brown and Higgs. And there was Pierce the under-gardener, whose condition was not likely to be coincidental to the current matter at hand.

"Are you warning us off?" I asked.

She smiled as though that was a ridiculous idea. "You're hired guns; you have to work to eat. But you're not… obsessed. When the boss man tells you to go ahead and open the box, maybe you'll have other ideas." She crossed her legs, a movement that absorbed Skinner's attention.

"You want us to carry on and find this thing," I said.

"Uh-huh." She placed two business cards in the middle of the table. "The number for my answering service is on the card. Call me anytime. You won't be sorry."

"Estelle De Vere, Psy. D." said the card, followed by the number and "Regent's Park 6425." Beneath was, "Theral Development Society."

"Is Psy. D to do with psychical research?"

"Nice try. But it's a psychology doctorate. Though psychology is closer to table rapping than you might think. You know what *theral* means?"

I shook my head.

"Whatever I want it to mean," she said, laughing at me with her eyes.

"Cormorant fishing," I said.

A tiny line appeared between her eyebrows. "Excuse me?"

"In China, instead of a rod and line or a net, the fishermen go out on a boat with ten or a dozen cormorants. You know the birds I mean?"

"It's like a cross between a crow and a duck," said Skinner.

"The cormorant dives down and catches fish. But the cunning Chinese put metal rings round their neck so they can't swallow, and when they come, up the fisherman takes the fish off them. The fisherman gets the fish, but the cormorant does all of the work."

She smiled for the first time. It was a memorable smile, warmer than I would have expected. "Yeah. That's about it. A man with a strong... motivation can find the things that nobody else can. You just have to follow them until they do. And that's how we get to Pandora's box first. Cormorant fishing."

If you hid a bottle from a drinker, he would tear the place apart looking for it and find things in places you could not even imagine. Stafford was like that, with that driven streak that meant he would keep on looking for his Holy Grail.

As we picked up the cards, she stubbed out her cigarette in an ashtray with a gesture of finality. "Now, I have a dinner date at the Ritz with one of your police commissioners." She did not sound as though she was looking forward to it. "He's going to tell me about criminal psychology. His wife is out of town. I'm sure it'll be fascinating."

"I'll walk you out," said Skinner.

She walked with an exaggerated gait on high heels, each step watched by every eye in the place.

"Now, she is what I call a real woman." Skinner sat down again, picking up the remaining card. "She had a limousine with a driver waiting for her, if you can believe that."

"I'm only surprised it wasn't an aeroplane."

"A real woman," he repeated. To me, though, Miss De Vere was unreal. She did not seem to be the same flesh and blood as us. It was impossible to think that she sweated and stank as we did, that she ate human food or had bodily functions. She was more like a projection or something out of a dream.

Chapter Nine

Expulsion from Eden

The three female librarians were in a huddle around the enquiries desk. From their postures and strained expressions, I divined that there was some difficulty. When I asked for Mr Hoade, they looked at each other before one of them responded.

"He's in the Reading Room. He'll be back in a minute."

I made my way to the far side of the building, where a contretemps was in progress. Mr Hoade, being the male, had been sent to deal with a rowdy patron. While understandable, that was a flawed strategy. Some of those lady librarians could freeze water at thirty paces with a look. They could easily quell a man who would have been honour-bound to stand up to a male librarian.

And so it proved. Hoade was remonstrating with a character with slicked-back hair and a dirty collar. The man had been tearing out pieces from the newspaper, probably the Situations Vacant column.

"This is a public library," hissed Hoade. "And I am asking you to leave."

"I know it's a public library," said the other in a barrack-room voice. "And I'm a member of the public! I've got every right to be here—I pay your wages. You can't push me around!"

Some of the others, fellow members of the unemployed, gave a murmur of assent. Nobody liked an officious librarian, and the paper tearer was obviously considered a wit in their circle.

"You keep your voice down," said Hoade, "and I won't ask you again to leave."

"Oh, won't you? That'll be a relief. 'Cause I'm not going."

That brought a burst of laughter from the onlookers.

"Shall I talk to this gentleman?" I asked.

Hoade jumped, surprised by my presence. I do move quietly at times.

"What an excellent idea," he said, rubbing his hands together. "I'll go and attend to matters in the reference section."

I took a step towards the loud-voiced man, moving not too close but close enough to loom over him. "Fun's over. You—hop it," I said quietly.

He looked round his audience with an expression that said, *Now, what do we have here?*

"Me—public; this—public library," he said, leaning back in his chair. "Get your zookeeper to explain it."

There was another burst of tittering.

"If you lay a finger on me, I'll have the law on you," he added. "Besides, what's it got to do with you?"

He knew better than to offer physical resistance. He "knew his rights," as his sort always did, and he was daring me to put myself in the wrong. While I hesitated, he would try to humiliate me by verbal means. The spectacle of a big man made to look foolish and tongue-tied was a popular attraction, as I knew all too well.

On that occasion, though, I was already on the front foot and laid into him verbally. "Our public library is an important national institution. It makes books and other reading material available to the likes of you and me. It's a treasure house of education, a fount of helpful instruction and information, an invaluable and inexhaustible stock for the schoolboy and the workingman alike. It is a great golden staircase of knowledge that is wide enough for all to climb upwards together."

"Is that so?" he said, taken slightly aback.

"Around us is gathered the wisdom of the great minds of the ages, the collected knowledge of all the world, classified by the latest scientific methods. Libraries are the cornerstone of our British civilisation. This is our heritage. This is all we have achieved in the world, these books here. The library is the concrete manifestation of all we hold most dear: democracy, culture, and the free expression of ideas."

"You sound like you've swallowed an encyclopaedia," was all he could mutter. It was a lame retort, and he knew it.

"An assault on the library is an attack on the fabric of our nation, and the library deserves to be defended with full force. So the likes of you can stay out of it until you learn to treat the institution with the respect it deserves."

On that last line, I put both hands on the chair legs, hoisted it into the air with him still sitting there, and shouldered it.

"Hey!" he protested, clinging to the seat with both hands.

"I haven't laid a finger on you." I proceeded to march to the main door.

He did not make much fuss. If he attacked me, I could simply drop him. Nor did he shout; there were few words more humiliating for a grown man to utter than "put me down." He did not draw attention to his unceremonious ejection.

Someone politely opened the door for me. I stepped outside and tipped my passenger out, placing the chair behind me. I did not want him coming in again.

"You think you're clever," he said, turning to face me.

Like many another, he thought that a surprise attack would give him all the advantage he needed. I could see the kick coming a mile off just from the way he altered his stance to deliver it. A boot to the groin was hardly the most original move. People seemed to think that because I was a boxer, I had no notion of defending against anything unless it was in the Marquis of Queensberry's rules.

As he kicked out, I stepped back smartly and caught his foot at the height of the kick. I held it in both my hands, with his leg fully extended, while he struggled vainly, and I looked at him reproachfully.

He managed to pull his foot loose, leaving me holding his shoe.

"Ha-ha!" he said.

"Ho-ho," said I and lobbed the shoe onto the back of a passing dustcart.

The lout looked at his shoe disappearing down the road. He swore at me more than necessary and ran after the dustcart, with a hobbling gait, on one stocking-clad foot.

An old man with a walking stick, who had paused to watch the fracas, shook his head disapprovingly. "That's no good. A fellow your size should have taught him a proper lesson for fighting dirty like that and given him a good hiding."

The public always wanted a good fight. I shrugged apologetically and, as the lout receded farther down the High Street in pursuit of his disappearing shoe, returned to the library with the chair. A man in a ragged shirt gave me a look. I suspected he was one of the lout's supporters, and when I scowled at him, he scuttled off.

Skinner said I should use my scowl more.

Mr Hoade seemed pleased to see me. "A very interesting discovery. The Knyght's Head is so called not after a generic knight, as you might have expected with a public house, but after a certain Mr Knyght, whose family owned land here in the sixteenth century. This is the same man that Knight's Hill is named for."

He polished his glasses, keeping me waiting for a denouement.

"Apparently, his decapitated body was found nearby, this being after a dispute with another local worthy, Sir Robert Harcourt. So the 'Knyght's Head' is in the nature of a macabre pun."

I was disappointed, but then he gave his little smile, eyes twinkling, and I saw that, in his own way, he had been joking, teasing me with that meaningless titbit.

Hoade's real discovery was something far more important. "But perhaps you're more interested in this." He wrote out on a slip of paper the letters *B-A-E-T-Y-L*. "Pronounced, more or less, 'beetle.' The OED came to the rescue, as usual."

"But what does it mean?"

"*Baetyl,* from the Latin *baetulus,* from the ancient Greek *baitulos,*" Hoade recited. "Pliny the Elder used the Latin word *betuli* specifically to distinguish round stones from oblong ones, which he termed *ceraunioi*. Baetyl, beetle—it's the right word. It comes from Greek, and it refers to something small and valuable that would fit the description."

"So a baetyl is a stone?"

"A rough stone. Specifically, a stone with a soul. A sacred stone hurled down from the heavens, one that is worshipped as a god. In practical terms, it refers to a stone that is, or rather is believed to be, a meteorite or aerolite. They were not uncommon as idols in the Greek and Semitic world."

"A meteorite," I said.

"Unfortunately, there's nothing more than that on our shelves here. But I've put in requests for the relevant textbooks from our other branches."

"That's very good of you."

"It's my job." Hoade spoke almost emotionlessly, but I thought I detected a ring of pride. "I was looking at your previous borrowings from the reference library in Upper Norwood, and you appear to have rather eclectic interests—Antarctic exploration, alchemy, theosophy, Chinese history, and now ancient religion. Though not boxing, which I gather is your particular area of expertise. As our friend in the Reading Room no doubt discovered."

When I gaped, he added, "I wondered if you might be a sportsman, and there is indeed a 'Stubbs, H' recorded in the annals." It was a small display of his prowess.

"I suppose I would be," I said.

I guessed that when Hoade was bored, he looked things up to entertain himself as easily as Skinner might whittle a stick. It was alarming that my history could be so easily uncovered. An interested person might be able to reconstruct my activities from my reading record. That might be dangerous if someone like Hoade was working for an enemy.

"I also noted from our records that you read a considerable quantity of fiction," Hoade added.

That made it sound as though I was a fantasist, living in a world of my own imagination. Skinner joked about my wanting to be John Hannay or Bulldog Drummond or Nayland Smith. He thought their adventures were childish stuff, a view that did him no credit but one many people shared.

"I have a weakness for works of imaginative fiction," I said.

"Don't apologise for it!" said Hoade, sounding more critical than ever. "Reference is the great, universal engine of the library, the powerhouse of raw knowledge. But literature—what you call imaginative fiction—is the embodiment of our wildest dreams. What is life for if you can't dream? How can a man discover anything without imagination to draw on?"

I was saved from having to answer the knotty literary question by the arrival of Skinner himself. He appeared behind Hoade, waving urgently and mouthing, "Come now." I excused myself and went after Skinner, and when I stepped outside, I found he was in a taxi parked up on the kerb with the door open.

"We've had an invitation to attend another of his Lordship's garden parties," said Skinner. "There's no dress code, so just hop in."

En route, I relayed what I had discovered concerning meteorites and baetyls.

Skinner nodded thoughtfully, smoothing his moustache. "Good work! That ought to narrow the search down at the Horniman. They can't have too many meteorites in their collection, can they?"

"I would assume not," I said though that was a pure guess on my part. The more I learned, the more things I discovered I knew nothing about.

I was still mulling this over as we turned down the avenue that led to the Firs.

"Once more into the breach, Harry," said Skinner.

Stafford was waiting at the gate with a shotgun slung over his shoulder, the young footman two paces behind him, and he looked wearily resigned. "Pierce got free. Don't worry; he's not wild the way he was last time. But he's… erratic. I thought we were better safe than sorry, so I called you."

The shotgun was a plain one with a cherry stock burnished by years of polishing. This was a favourite shooting gun, not just the first one that came to hand. The situation had become almost routine.

"Very wise, sir," said Skinner.

"I got you the rope, the sack, and the gloves," said the footman, holding up these items to Skinner. His right hand was wrapped in a neat white bandage.

"Good man," said Skinner, drawing on a glove and flexing his fingers. "Same drill as last time, then, Mr Stubbs."

"He's over by the fountain," said Stafford.

The old gardener was keeping an eye on the madman from a distance. Pierce was wearing the same clothes as before and crouching over a flowerbed. He was thin and wasted, and his corpse-like pallor showed no improvement.

Close up, he looked far worse. His skin was wrinkled up with the texture of towelling. Normally, a sick man's skin would tighten over the bones and his features would take on a harsher relief, but Pierce's face seemed less distinct as though the sharp lines were being worn away like a weathered statue.

"You just leave that and come indoors a bit now," the old gardener was saying. "You know it ain't good for you to be outside in the sun."

"I can't stand it." Pierce's voice was horribly changed to a rasping whisper. He was plucking weeds from the flowerbed with short, agitated movements. There were quite a few weeds, more than there had been previously. He looked down at them with dismay. "I want to get back, but it's all different. We are all different."

"Maybe we can help you, lad," said Skinner.

Pierce turned round stiffly and looked up at us from a thousand miles away. "I'm the under-gardener. I'm keeping these weeds down, but we don't understand."

Skinner made a small gesture, signalling the rest of us to spread out and surround the boy. We moved slowly and carefully so as not to startle him as if approaching a frightened horse.

"All we want is for you to get better," said Skinner soothingly.

"Me, me, me," said Pierce. "Who am I? Do you know who I am?"

"You're the under-gardener," said Skinner.

"I am Legion!" said Pierce with sudden vehemence, slapping his own forehead. "Too many of us. Too many in one head! I just want to work in the garden, but I don't know who we are any more."

He turned to the flowerbed and started pulling weeds with great energy, ripping them out of the ground one after the other.

"We could just let him carry on until he's exhausted," said Skinner. "Or would you prefer to bring this to a close?"

"Get him back inside," said Stafford.

"Too many weeds," said Pierce, working down the row. "Weeds in my head. Legion, legion of weeds. Pluck 'em out; pluck 'em all out!"

At Skinner's signal, the two of us stepped briskly forward. Pierce leapt up like a frog, away from Skinner and slap-bang into me. He looked surprised as I took his arms and forced them behind him. This time there was no real struggle. I belatedly realised that what I took to be resistance was just the calcified stiffness of his limbs, which only bent in some directions. It took him a while to straighten his legs to stand up, and it was difficult for him to get his arms behind his back. Once we had got over that difficulty, he was secured in short order.

Pierce continued to mumble throughout, but at the end, he looked up, and the real man shone through like the sun coming from behind a cloud.

"It's all my fault," he told Skinner. "Don't let them blame Evie for this."

"Keep her out of this!" yelled the footman, throwing himself at Pierce. He would have hit the under-gardener if I had not stepped in between and restrained him. Skinner, meanwhile, kept hold of the unresisting Pierce.

"Let's just calm down now," said Stafford to the footman. It was a milder rebuke than I might have expected.

The footman looked away shamefacedly, and Skinner and the old gardener frogmarched Pierce back to the house at a funeral pace.

There was something white on the ground; I thought it was slug in the flowerbed. It was a human digit. There was no blood, but the end of it looked soft and crumbly, more like fresh clay than flesh and bone. It was Pierce's thumb. He did not even seem to have noticed the loss. The whole thing was profoundly disturbing. A few weeks since, Pierce had been a fit, healthy young man; now he was a shambling wreck in mind and body, literally falling apart.

"Nobody else in the household affected?" I casually asked Stafford, having drawn his attention to the thumb.

"Nobody," said Stafford. "And with Pierce… it's not as bad as it looks."

A good officer never needed to explain anything to his subordinates and certainly never needed to apologise. Stafford was not a good officer. Nor was I a good enough actor to pretend I believed him. As I struggled for polite words, he spoke first.

"It's not a notifiable illness," said Stafford. "I give you my word. It's not infectious at all. It was an accident." He continued to try to justify himself. "I told you there was another source. A gipsy woman brought me some water."

"Water?"

"Water from the Grail," said Stafford. "She warned me. And I warned the staff not to touch it on any account. Young Pierce took it into his head to try drinking it."

"Why?" I asked.

Stafford shook his head. "One of the maids dared him, and the damn fool went ahead and did it to impress her."

I had read up a little on the Holy Grail, which was a sort of cup with mystic healing properties. I wondered whether the servants knew something about Stafford's quest to find it. It was hard to believe they did not have any inkling. But the Grail was not supposed to be harmful—quite the opposite.

"A little would have been safe," said Stafford as though following my thoughts. "It was the quantity he took. 'The dose makes the poison,' you know."

"Is there a treatment?"

"It'll work its way out of his system in a few more days," Stafford said without any great conviction.

"We have a lead in the matter of Mabel Brown," I said just to change the subject. I explained about how the beetle was a baetyl, and therefore a meteorite, somewhere in the Horniman's collection. Skinner came jauntily up the path before I was finished.

"Good work," said Stafford at my conclusion. He had

been less surprised than I had expected and had asked fewer questions. It was as though I was simply confirming something and he had known about the baetyl all along.

"Let me know how you progress. Do you need more money?"

"Not at present, sir," said Skinner. "But I'll be sure to let you know when we do."

"Good, good. Look, we really are getting somewhere here, and you've been an absolute credit. Just–bear with me. We'll keep a better eye on Pierce, but stand ready. In the next few days, I may have a rather tricky piece of work for you connected with our second source."

He bit his lip as if he might have said too much. Stafford was balanced between enthusiasm and anxiety. He never shared any more information with us than he had to. That had always puzzled me before; we were his loyal confederates and deeply implicated in his schemes, and it would have seemed in his best interests to keep us well informed. Even the army told a soldier what he needed to know to carry out an operation.

But his worry was the eternal worry of the miser and the hoarder. Stafford was concerned that if we knew too much, we would take the prize for ourselves. He assumed that we must be as enthused as he was over his Grail in spite of all we had seen. He could not bring himself to trust even us.

"We're ever at your service, sir," said Skinner.

Pleased again, Stafford dismissed us, and we marched back to the gate. We both tried not to stare at the new greenhouse next to the potting shed. A few days earlier, there had just been shoots two inches long. Now the vegetation inside was so thick and lush that it pressed on the glass as though ready to burst out. It could have been an advertisement for a miracle fertiliser except that there was something unwholesome about the growth as if the superabundance was nourished by a sewage outfall.

The leaves did not seem right. The packed greenery behind the steam-fogged glass looked more like tentacled seaweed than honest land plants. Was it an illusion, or did they wave? Stafford's Grail water was being put to use, growing, I did not doubt, the golden apples of the sun. I wondered whether they would take their form from our sun or from an alien star.

Chapter Ten

A Trip to the Museum

A letter from Sally arrived in the office the next day while I was in conference with Skinner, filling him in on what I had discovered on the beetle question.

"Mr Stubbs—this is just to let you know Miss De Vere upped sticks and left this morning with no notice. She has not left a proper forwarding address just a post office. Anything I hear I will pass on. Miss Berry was put out. Yrs, Sally."

"Perhaps she was summoned away on important business for her Theral Development Society," I said.

I had asked Hoade to look it up, and he had informed me that no such organisation existed, or at least not officially. Which did not surprise me greatly.

"She didn't have any reason to stay after Mabel Brown combusted," said Skinner. "That rooming house wasn't exactly her class of place. Now, about beetles and this Roman emperor...?"

"Emperor Heliogabulus, otherwise known as Elegabulus, was famed for his eccentric and vicious ways," I said, reading from my notebook. "Allegedly, he once had enemies smothered to death with rose petals."

To my surprise, Skinner burst into song: "I quote in elegiacs all the crimes of Heliogabalus... " Then he stopped and indicated for me to go on.

"He got his name from a cult he belonged to that worshipped a meteorite, this itself also having the name of Elagabal. When he became Emperor, Heliogabulus had the stone brought to Rome, where it was paraded through the city on a chariot drawn by six horses and installed in a brand-new temple."

"Very grand, I'm sure." Skinner had his knife out; he had previously carved his initials in the tabletop and now proceeded to add curlicues to the letters.

"In 210 BC," I said, "when Rome was threatened by Hannibal, the senate pleaded that another baetyl be brought to the city to defend them. King Attalus of Persia duly gave them a stone that was identified with the goddess known as the *magna mater*, or Great Mother. Who is also variously known as Cybele and Astarte—a goddess still worshipped secretly to this day by some gipsies."

I was pleased by this link to Stafford's gipsy woman, but Skinner was unimpressed. "Oh, yes," he said offhandedly. "I know Magna Mater, that old baggage. But is this strictly cogent to the matter in hand?"

He had no very great interest in the wider considerations, whereas I believed that only by a careful accumulation of knowledge could we can make sense of things.

I skimmed over accounts of other ancient baetyls, all painstakingly gleaned from the books supplied by Hoade. Some sacred meteorites were inert, but others were livelier and exercised a control over their worshippers through dreams and visions. They popped up all over the place in different religions. The fabled Black Stone at Mecca was supposed to be a meteorite. Jacob's dream of a ladder to heaven came when his head was pillowed on a rock; he decided the rock was a sacred gift from heaven, assumed by some scholars to indicate a meteorite. Jacob founded a temple there, calling the place Beth-el—which some said was the root of the word *baetyl*. Other equally learned men said all that was rubbish.

"There's no consistency," I said, "in the description of the meteorites themselves in terms of colour, size, or shape. Also, they have a tendency to disappear over time and be replaced with copies."

"And that's all your book learning can tell us, then?"

"I've made all the running here," I said, not having mentioned Hoade's role. "You needn't look down your nose at me, not when you haven't done anything."

"Not so, my Titanic friend," said Skinner, with an irritating air of self-congratulation. He drew out a folder with some loose papers. "I will give you your baetyls, but you must give me necrocomica." He spoke the last word with relish. "That being a term coined by none other than our old friend Paracelsus for exactly what you're talking about: mystic meteorites. Some say Paracelsus wrote a book about them, the *Liber Necrocomicon*. I never turned up a copy, but I spent a good deal of time chasing round second-hand—pardon me, *antiquarian*—bookshops, on behalf of a certain gentleman I could name." He looked up from the papers. "If you ever want to feel like a proper Charlie, try going round asking for a book that never existed and having every know-it-all book peddler put you right."

"But if he never wrote it…?"

"I can still tell you a meteorite came down outside the city of Ensisheim in 1492," said Skinner, reading from his notes. "Which Kaiser Maximilian claimed was a miracle from God. He ordered the stone to be hung up in chains from the church ceiling, which it duly was and where it remains to this day."

"And that might be what we're looking for?"

"Not a bit of it. Paracelsus examined that one in 1528, and he didn't reckon there was much to it. Said it was made of earthly material and not a miraculous heavenly substance like dear old Kaiser Max claimed. Some meteorites are just ordinary stones, and some of them, according to Paracelsus, are not. It never occurred to me that it might be connected with this beetle until you made the association."

"Some meteorites draw lightning," I said thoughtfully. "They fly through the heavens, where our patron can see them with his telescope, and they spit out shooting stars like a ship dropping boats to land on an island. And when they land, they become gods or at least baetyls."

Skinner shrugged. It was all one to him. "And all we need to do is find where the Horniman Museum keeps their collection of baetyls or necrocomica or mystic meteorites. We look for the one that Mabel Brown chipped a bit off of, and we make them an offer for it. Easy as pie."

Skinner did not seem troubled by other aspects of the case, such as Pierce the gardener being the victim of some accident. I forbore to ask whether he would be buying the baetyl on behalf of our patron or Dr Estelle De Vere. Instead, by mutual consent, we donned our hats and set out to catch the bus for Lordship Lane to visit a place I had not been to since my schooldays before the war.

The Horniman Museum was a local landmark, an expansive edifice in light-grey stone with something of the temple and something of the castle about it. It had a square clock tower like a church with a circular top to it, and the rest of it was like a series of Greek temples with pillars—or railways stations if you looked at it in that way. The man who built it was the founder of Horniman Tea, who grew very rich from being the first to sell tea in small packets, rather than in larger parcels that the grocer would have to draw from like sugar or flour.

Horniman collected items from around the world while doing business, and the collection outgrew his house. Being wealthy, he had a museum built for it, and like every local schoolboy, I found it a place of wonder and mystery. There was a stuffed walrus the size of an elephant at the entrance, sitting on an artificial iceberg, like the guardian of the gates to another world, with tusks like ivory scimitars. The walrus was a great, bloated beast, intimidating, looking at visitors all glass eyed. Guides loved to tell children how the beast killed Eskimos, rearing up and dragging their kayaks under the icy water and eating them when it mistook them for seals. I remember one boy fainted when he heard that. It wasn't me, I should add.

"Mr Horniman set out to bring the whole world here," Skinner needlessly told me. "It stands to reason that if there's anything you want from anywhere in the world, especially if it's a bit hocus-pocus, it's probably in there somewhere."

The museum still looked like a fair-sized haystack to my eyes, and the baetyl was a small enough needle, but there was no sense in arguing with Skinner when he was in a cheerful mood.

"Maybe we were wrong about what sort of beetle it is," said Skinner as we came into the first gallery.

Along the walls were hundreds and hundreds of glass display cases, and in them was every insect imaginable, so many that from a distance they looked like writing on the wall. The insect gallery was like framed collections of pinned butterflies but multiplied to infinity. Or perhaps multiplied to insanity.

There were butterflies of every colour of the rainbow and more than a few other insects, but mainly, there was a vaster profusion of beetles than I'd ever imagined existed. Many of them were extraordinary creatures, giants the size of a cricket balls or small monsters equipped with all manner of appendages and extrusions so that the row of them was a carpenter's shop of tools for boring, sawing, or filing through wood. Many more were unremarkable brown beetles that were utterly indistinguishable to the naked eye. Somebody could tell them apart though, and each one had a neatly printed tag with its Latin name. Most of them never even had an English name.

"What's it all for?"

"Collectors," said Skinner. "They start out just collecting the fancy colourful ones. Then the collecting mania takes over, and look what happens."

"They want the complete set." But the complete set of beetles was... colossal. I wondered how anyone could even know if they had the same beetle twice—or how they could tell when they really had completed the set. If there was a reference guide, it was in the sole possession of the Creator. Dizzied by this vast multitude, I retreated to another gallery.

This one held West African artefacts. My eyes ranged over a bronze idol with straw for hair, a wooden statue of a man with the head of a crocodile, a woven straw mat, and a ceremonial staff with ornate bronze furniture. The descriptions on the printed cards were terse and uninformative.

Skinner had decided that rather than asking the staff directly, he would get assistance from the other visitors. He stubbed out his cigarette and straightened his tie. The first three people he approached knew nothing, but Skinner was persistent, and his eyes lit up when a likely prospect appeared. A gentleman was showing his son around the gemstone collection. The boy had slicked-back hair and a school blazer and seemed genuinely interested as his father explained the finer points. The father used Greek and Latin terms with a great deal of familiarity. Skinner approached them, speaking up in an accent that was a poor imitation of the man's own rounded tones.

"Awf'ly sorry to bother you, but you don't happen to know where the meteorite collection is displayed, do you?"

"Meteorites?" The amateur mineralogist turned to the boy. "I don't think we've seen any, do you?"

The boy shook his head, and his father extracted a museum catalogue. I had not even seen them on sale.

"I understood there were some interesting specimens of meteorites," said Skinner.

"I dare say," replied the scholar. "But I'm afraid there's nothing listed."

"I must have been misinformed. Dashed sorry to trouble you and all that."

"As I say, I'm sure they have got some interesting specimens," said the other man. "But you'll have a devil of a time finding them. I mean, look at this."

The display case in front of him held an arrangement of yellow crystals from different parts of the world. Some were clear and pale and the size of my thumbnail, and others were the size and brilliant hue of egg yolks.

"They've arranged them by colour!" He laughed and looked to see if we understood the joke. Having different yellow stones next to each other gave a person a chance to compare them and tell them apart, but that was evidently not the way to do it at all.

"Bit of a shambles, eh?" said Skinner, still in his plummy accent.

"It's a junk shop, an absolute junk shop. You see, this is what happens when you have an amateur collector with no sense of scientific organisation." His conviction was total; I would not like to be an underling who misplaced something in that man's business.

"Hopeless," Skinner said.

A young couple joined us to listen; the scholar was holding forth, and they wanted to hear the free lecture.

"And then all these other collectors started offloading their collections on him, and Horniman just took everything," said the mineral scholar. "So instead of having some sense of order, you have red-Indian feather headdresses, Mongolian snakes, and African bronzes with no rhyme or reason. I'm sure it's all very *entertaining* for the public, but it's worthless for educational purposes."

"I suppose we'll just have to forage for the meteorites," said Skinner.

"I very much doubt that will do you any good," said the other in the cheery tone of a railwayman telling you that the 7:15 had already left. "Nine-tenths of the collection isn't on show; it's packed away in storage."

"The Horniman Museum has over two hundred thousand individual objects," said the boy. "Most of them are in storage, but sometimes they lend them to other museums and galleries all over the world."

"And they haven't even catalogued it all properly yet," said the scholar. "You see, I was talking to a friend of mine—friend of a colleague, actually, from South Africa—and he was visiting because his uncle had donated some very fine rhodochrisite—"

"Pink manganese carbonate," said the boy as if providing footnotes. He was doubtless the class swot.

"We couldn't find it on display, and when I made enquiries, they hadn't even opened the boxes! Can you believe it?"

"Scarcely," said Skinner, bowing and withdrawing before the man could continue. "Very glad for your assistance."

I carried on down the aisle, studiously reading the little labels like an explorer searching for tracks in the wasteland. Skinner followed but looked around in wider arcs.

"Hello," he muttered. "Don't look now, but you see that cove with the bowed legs?"

I had noticed the man before. He had the face of a ferret and wore a jacket that showed its age and scuffed brown shoes. He kept about half a hall away, but he was always there. He looked shifty and out of place, glancing from exhibit to exhibit or staring for too long at some dull display. The museum was not his natural habitat. Whichever way he looked, he never looked in our direction.

"Is he following us?" I asked.

"We'll soon find out. Let's nab him."

Skinner and I wandered around until we found a gallery of Asian art with no other visitors. When the ferret-faced man followed us in a minute later, we ambushed him from either side of the doorway. I took his right arm and bent it behind him in a half nelson. He was a powerful enough man for his size, but breaking a hold like that required more than strength.

I had not seen Skinner draw his knife, but it was at the man's cheek in an instant. A thin line of blood appeared where the sharp blade touched the skin.

"What's your game?"

The man said nothing but glared with mute hostility.

"What do you think you're doing in a museum?" Skinner jeered. "You stand out like a sore thumb."

He glared at us silently.

"You got anything to say for yourself, or shall I cut your ear to match Mr Stubbs's?"

I was fairly certain Skinner was bluffing. He sounded convincing, though.

"There's no law against following someone," the ferret-faced man burst out. "I haven't done anything to you."

"Why don't you go back to Miss Granger," said Skinner, voice low and silky with menace, "and give her our best compliments. Because if we ever catch you in a quiet place again, she'll get you back by instalments. You have my word on that."

Skinner withdrew the blade and nodded; I threw the man down the aisle between cabinets so that he fetched up against the wooden panelling. I was terrified he would smash into something glass and break it, but I bowled him cleanly.

"Poor bleeder," said Skinner, half-scornful and half-pitying, as the man slunk out. He had the awkward, limping gait of one who had survived rickets as a boy. Evidently, Elsie Granger had not given up her interest in the beetle and still thought there was a chance of profit.

"He's like us only not as well paid," I said.

"Clever, though. If a man's unemployed and loitering anyway, he must be very cheap to hire. And she can pay them in watered-down beer. I thought I saw someone loitering outside the office yesterday."

"There might have been one in the library," I said, recalling the man in the ragged shirt. "Perhaps he knows that we're here after the beetle. But he doesn't know what sort of a beetle it is."

Even as I said it, I wondered whether our shadow might have been close enough to overhear Skinner's enquiry about meteorites.

"It's got to be in here somewhere," said Skinner, scanning the rows of cabinets.

"That note was a clue. The one I found in the book in Mabel Brown's room—'Janitor, archivist, master key held where?'"

"She had to get a key to wherever it was in here."

"Or in the archive storage," I said.

"Why couldn't she leave a note saying where it was?" Skinner grumbled.

The museum was not even as well organised as Higgs's warehouse, where all the men's shoes were on one table. If only the museum had been as neatly ordered as Mr Hoade's library shelves, all sorted and classified and numbered according to the guiding principles of the Dewey Decimal System and drawn up in parade-ground order on the shelves for inspection.

"We need help from an expert," I said.

Chapter Eleven

On Streatham Common

Hoade smoothed his beard contemplatively. I was lucky to find him free, Saturday morning being a busy time for any library. But he had granted me a minute in a quiet corner, and we were deep in conference.

I had doubled back on myself a couple of times on the way to the library to make sure I had not been followed. Skinner might sneer at my correspondence course, but it does give some handy tips on avoiding surveillance.

"It beggars belief that Mabel Brown should have found this baetyl fortuitously." Hoade chewed on an unlit pipe. "Given how soon she found it and succeeded in abstracting a sample, I'd incline to the view that she knew what she was looking for when she joined the museum. Moreover, she must have had some idea of how to find it."

"But how?" I asked.

"We must assume that the item is in one box among ten thousand other boxes. Either she had some means of sniffing it out, or she had some inside information on where to look."

"The baetyl does have unique physical properties. That may well include smell, so perhaps a dog would be able to smell it—"

"I was speaking metaphorically," said Hoade with that tight smile of his. Another man would have laughed. "I was thinking more in terms of magnetic or electric properties. If the baetyl draws lightning, then it may have some characteristic effect on a compass needle or similar. But of course you are correct. It might indeed also have a characteristic smell."

I also wondered whether radiation might be involved and if that could be detected. There was nothing in Mabel Brown's room that suggested a scientific instrument or even an interest in it.

"As for inside information," he went on, "there are only a finite number of people with any knowledge of the contents of those boxes and a finite number of places where they might have broadcast the information and where she might have encountered it. Only certain academic researchers would be permitted to browse through the collection, and there are only a few journals that publish their papers."

"Is there a journal of baetyl studies?" I was thinking that perhaps some small monograph on, for example, the discovery of an unusual baetyl in Arctic Russia would point the way. Being the subject of an obscure study should be enough for the find to merit its own display case at least.

"I think it's something more rarefied than that," Hoade said. "Perhaps some reference in a paper on something else—a hint that would point the way for the informed student."

"But how would you even start to look for such a thing?"

The rows and rows of books and the mass of bound copies of magazines stretching down shelf after shelf, each packed with pages of dense text, seemed to grow around me into a vast and impenetrable forest in which I had to find one particular acorn—an acorn I would not even be able to recognise when I found it.

"The modern librarian has many tools at his disposal," said Hoade, a kindly wizard ready to assist an awed petitioner. "Systematic searching is a now scientific process, not merely a matter of intuition. But we will need to gather all the clues and decide which trail offers the most promise."

I dutifully wrote about all the pieces of evidence, and Hoade promptly rearranged them according to some scheme of his own. He ended up with six points, which he frowned at critically as he drew lines and arrows between them. It might have been scientific, or he might have been casting runes, but after a minute, he seemed decided.

"I would say the history of the Horniman Museum offers

the best prospects," he said. "Being local, we probably have as good a collection of books on the Horniman as anyone."

"What are we looking for?"

"I'm afraid I will have to defer my answer until Monday," Hoade said, looking up at the big clock over the reception desk. "I have a few things to attend to before we close up. But you need not despair, Stubbs. We will find the track—I'm sure of that—even if we don't make it to the destination in one go."

"It's very good of you." I hesitated. I needed to warn him. "But I do feel that I should warn you... this is a dangerous business to get caught up in. Even the books themselves might turn against you."

"How so?"

I shuffled awkwardly. I had not thought properly about how I was going to put this. "I don't rightly understand the process, but some minds—some educated minds—are vulnerable to certain occult things. They'd pass right by someone like me, but they could be swallowed like a fishhook to someone who was susceptible."

I did not know what drove people like Stafford or Harcourt or Roslyn D'Onston, but it always seemed to start with people reading books and letting ideas get lodged in their brains. And there was something of that type of temperament in Hoade.

"Like becoming addicted to cross-words," Hoade said lightly. "Only more so."

"I suppose so," I said, but I saw from his sober expression that he understood me. Perhaps he already understood more than I would have given him credit for. Hoade was a man who knew things.

"Thank you for your concern. Forewarned is forearmed. I will shun the snares of the occult and see you on Monday morning. Have a pleasant weekend, Stubbs."

"And yourself."

"In-laws," he said with a brief, resigned smile.

My heart was lightened considerably by his optimism that we would find something. I was inclined to trust Hoade when he was dealing with matters that he understood better than me.

It was a beautiful Saturday afternoon. I had promised to join my family for a promenade around Streatham Common. There were seven of us all told: my pa and ma, my brother and his wife, little George, aged three, and the baby in a perambulator. Skinner had taken himself off to Tooting Bec Lido, where he would meet some friends to ogle the season's bathing belles.

On days when the sun beat down, all London went out of doors. The footpaths were crowded with throngs of pale-skinned folks, looking like underground creatures let out into the light of day for the first time in their summer clothes, all smelling of mothballs. The young men got spruced up in their straw hats and striped blazers and thought they were terrific sports. They'd walk four or five abreast, the formation opening and all hats swept off when they met their female counterparts coming the other way, who were all floral and dainty and trying to stay aloof behind fans and parasols. Then they'd burst into fits of giggles when they were ten paces past the boys.

Streatham Common was a cheerful sight that summer's day. The kids were all shouting and running around and being organised into games of cricket by proud fathers. The mothers looked after the little ones and spread out tartan blankets and unpacked wicker baskets full of provender. Here and there, if you looked for them, young couples were finding shady arbours and quiet corners or just walking holding hands and looking soppy.

It was all so green at this time of year—the vast expanse of grass, the rows of hedges, and the fine oaks at the top of the common—that I had to stop and wonder what colour it had been a few weeks previously. The same green, I supposed, but it did not show it without the sunshine. The whole surface of the ground was covered in green, vegetation spreading like a liquid that filled every nook and cranny with fresh verdant growth. It was the sort of day that made me think I spent too much time indoors.

A team of workmen were driving in posts, roping off the bottom end of the common by the fountain, preparing the area for the summer fair that would set up there in the coming week. We sauntered along, taking it in, talking about nothing much at all. Pa was content to be flanked by his sons and surrounded by the rest of his family. My brother was also more cheerful of late. Being a die-hard fan of Crystal Palace Football Club, he had spent his Saturday afternoons watching them endure a string of losses ending in relegation. The season had ended, and my brother could break loose from being part of the great collective of Crystal Palace fans and spend time with his family. Sport in the summer months meant Jack Hobbs knocking out endless centuries, which held no interest.

We had reached the Rookery, a series of gardens and sweeping views at the top of the common. An Italian was selling ices from a handcart; I proposed getting one for everyone, and my brother and I joined the queue.

Georgie needed a farthing for the wishing well. Back in the last century, the place had been famous for its mineral waters. It had been a sort of health resort for Londoners, and nearby Beulah Spa had once been a fashionable spot where they came to take the waters. But springs came and went at their own whim, and all that remained on Streatham Common were a few old buildings and the wishing well.

"Tell him to use his wish wisely," I told my brother.

"Knowing him, he'll just wish for ice cream," he said.

My eye was caught by an unusually fine motorcar, a powder-blue limousine parked with two wheels up on the grass. The windows were rolled down for the occupants to enjoy the sunshine. In the back seat, wearing a pair of sunglasses—something I had only seen in pictures of Hollywood stars—was a beautiful woman with blond hair. Her bare arm, adorned with a gold bracelet, rested on the windowsill.

The dark glasses, round and shiny as insects' eyes, hid her expression entirely. I could not even see what direction she was looking in, and there was no sign she had seen me. But Miss De Vere had seen both me and my family, and she wanted me to know it. Of course, she had as much right to the common as anyone else, but I did not appreciate mute intimidation from any source, not when it involved my family.

"Excuse me one minute," I said to my brother. "I just need to attend to a small business matter."

I strode over with long steps and unclenched my fists with a deliberate effort. My first thought had been to go over and rock the car, threatening to turn it over. That would have shaken her up. But that would be childish and foolish. It would draw attention, and what possible excuse could I give for such an attack?

It would also mean a fight with her chauffeur. The man in the front seat was a substantial individual; the uniform did not conceal the thickness of his arms and neck. He sat at attention, eyes forward but alert.

Two paces later, I had thoughts of breaking off the wing mirror, but that was equally futile and would show the hopelessness of the physical approach.

As with the lout in the library, I would need to find a verbal counter.

Her head turned slowly as I approached. Diamonds on her bracelet sparkled in the sun.

"Do you have some business with me?" I demanded.

"Aw, and I thought you'd be flattered I'm here," she said, pouting. "Not many men get this sort of attention."

She was not exactly mocking, but superior. Skinner might, perhaps, have attempted to flirt with her. I was not in the mood.

"I have your business card, and I will contact you as and when I see appropriate. I don't welcome your attentions when they are directed at my family."

"Aw, hold your horses, cowboy," she said, or rather, drawled. "I'm not here to threaten your delightful family."

"Then why…?"

"I was honestly disappointed not to hear from you. You know… I could use a man like you on my side."

I sensed the driver's eyes on me in the wing mirror. It was half the look of a bodyguard assessing a threat, half the look of a jealous rival.

"My services have already been engaged by another employer," I said.

"You're aware that this particular Pandora's box contains an alien material. And it's dangerous."

She turned her head and looked down the hill, towards the horizon. Rainbow points of light danced from her bracelet.

For a moment, the quality of the sunlight shifted. I was still standing in front of her in the same pose, and the contours of the land were the same, but the common and the people had gone, and we were in the middle of a desert. Now she was in a carriage—I'm not sure what it looked like. I was watching the towering dust storm blowing towards us across the lifeless landscape. It was not quite a mirage or a dream, and it was so fleeting that I hardly had time to register the details. There were houses, but they were empty shells, and the church at the bottom of the hill was a ruin, and the city was all ruin that merged into dunes in the distance. I blinked, and the vision had gone. The greenery and the crowds had returned, and the noise came back like someone turning on a gramophone.

"Hypnosis," I said, wondering if it was the effect of her bracelet and looking around to reassure myself that everything was back in place. The vision, for all that it was fleeting, had the vividness of a nightmare. Roslyn D'Onston wrote about visions of the past and the future being conjured up and shared, but I had not thought the trick could be done in broad daylight.

"Hypnosis is a cheap trick," she said. "Freud talks about the human subconscious. The universe has a subconscious too. You just had a peek into it."

"I don't understand."

"Sure you do," she said with a complicit smile. "You can shove a man out of the way with physical force, or you can use psychology and persuade him to move. Same with the world. Magic is just psychology."

I suppose that some men, the sort who judge a woman by her looks, would assume that Miss De Vere was what Americans called a "dumb blond." The same people would assume I lacked intellect because of my physique. Miss De Vere and I had more in common than that, though. You might say that each of us had been born with certain natural gifts, and we had both improved upon nature, me with the goal of being a better fighter, and her to become… what? A siren, I supposed. Both of us quietly used our talents in pursuit of the extraordinary, dealing in matters that all those hundreds on Streatham Common would never believe.

And both of us were on the trail of the same dangerous quarry, which had fallen as a shooting star.

"What do you want from me?" I asked.

"This thing you're after, it runs through living things like a disease. It holds them together, and when it goes… they turn into dust."

"I thought it might be something like radioactivity," I said. "Like radium."

She raised an eyebrow. I was guessing, but perhaps she was surprised by the acuity of the guess. Or its inaccuracy.

"Well… the energy behind it is something like that. Altered matter, isomers rather than isotopes, but it'll burn you to dust either way." She smiled as she put me right. No doubt there were times when Miss De Vere had to hold her tongue and let others hold forth. But she was never going to let me imagine I knew more than her. "Think about what could happen if it gets loose. All these people… dust."

"I appreciate the concern," I said.

She leaned forward to tap her driver on the shoulder.

"I have a champagne picnic to attend in Dulwich Park," she said before looking up so her eyes met mine with sudden directness. Her voice dropped to a purr. "I know you and I can do business, Harry. There's a lot riding on it."

"I'll think about it," I said, my voice unexpectedly hoarse.

Looking at the hand that I had unconsciously placed on the car windowsill, she added, "Careful. You wouldn't want to lose a finger, now."

I lifted my hand, and the deep rumble of the limousine's engine drowned out any reply I might make. The car glided off, stately as a galleon.

"Now, she's a right fancy piece of work," commented my brother, having seen the transaction. "How do you know a woman like that?"

"She's a business acquaintance. She wants me to leave my employer and work for her."

"And she shows up here on a Saturday afternoon?" He looked at me with a new respect. "I won't ask you no questions about your business, and you don't need to tell me no lies."

"Mrs Blundell mentioned her daughter saw you in the tea shop with a woman the other day," said Ma.

"That was a different woman entirely," I said, which didn't make it sound any better. "An informant on a case I'm working on."

My mother waited to see whether I would reveal anything more, but I knew it was best to stay silent. If she found out who Sally was, and what her former profession had been, she would be mortified.

"It may be none of my business," said Ma, "but a mother likes to know."

Ma had views on potential wives. Her life was a round of sweeping, scrubbing, laundering, cooking, baking, darning, and knitting, not to mention shopping and running a household, and any woman who could not meet her exacting standards was not fit for the job. Luckily, my sister-in-law was from the same rugged, good-humoured stock. When the next Sunday roast was served, the white tablecloth would be perfectly ironed, the glasses polished to a gleam, and the Brussels sprouts cooked to within an inch of extinction, all according to unwritten regulation. My brother and I would be trusted with washing up afterwards but nothing else.

"He's not courting," my brother assured her. "Harry isn't situated for that sort of thing."

I had lacked any sort of steady employment ever since leaving Latham and Rowe. The job with the fictitious insurance company was certainly lucrative, but in Skinner's view, it was a short-term occupation with no prospects. The bubble could burst any day, and we had to make the most of it while we could. Our employment rested on a rich man's whim. If next week his wife persuaded him to take up breeding Afghan hounds instead of pursuing arcane knowledge, we would be out on the streets.

"Maybe in a year or two I'll be set up for courting," I said. "At the moment I'm still learning the trade – and I need to finish my correspondence course."

"I'd say your prospects are looking up," said my brother. "What a motor! What do you think—is it fifty horsepower? But

I liked the look of that Daimler your Chinese cove used to drive around."

"Who did you say that blond woman was?" persisted my mother.

"She's an American writer," I said. "Miss De Vere. She's come over here to write a book about English life."

My mother said nothing but pursed her lips. I could read her thoughts well enough. Nothing good could come from consorting with flashy American women however much money they might happen to have.

I wanted to tell her what Sally had said about Miss De Vere and how she and my mother would agree, but there was no way to bring the conversation around.

"A funny thing happened to me in the library this morning," I said.

Chapter Twelve

The Gipsy

I was back at the library first thing on Monday morning, entering beneath the watchful gaze of Shakespeare and his peers. True to his word, Hoade had found the answer. Or at least, so he thought: the exact details lay somewhere in the books spread out before me. It should have been easier to find a clue in those volumes than in the hundreds of thousands of items in the Horniman Museum's collection, but it was still no small undertaking.

At the same time, I had drawn some uncomfortable conclusions from my weekend conversation with Miss De Vere.

It was another lovely morning, and the rectangle of sunlight from the window had moved a good way round the office before Skinner arrived. He looked no better than usual for a Monday morning, peering at the world through a haze of hangover. His hair was combed tidily at the front, but the back bristled in all directions like an angry hedgehog. I had no sympathy for his sorry state.

"You talked to her," I said.

Skinner hung his hat on the rack and slung his jacket over the back of his chair, buying time while he struggled to get his misfiring brain into gear. "So what if I did?"

"You didn't mention it to me."

Skinner spread his hands in a show of openness. "After what we saw in that garden, it seemed best to explore our options."

He picked up the envelope on his desk and fed it back and forth through his fingers.

"She showed you the wasteland, did she?"

"Aha, so you've been talking to her too, have you? That's downright hypocritical."

"I didn't talk to her," I said. "She talked to me."

"She's not wrong, though, is she? Do you want to see this green and pleasant land"—he waved at the tree outside, whose leaves practically brushed the window—"turned into the ruddy Sahara Desert?"

"Bearing in mind the source, the credibility of that claim is open to question."

Skinner pulled up his chair and leaned close. "It's all science," he said as if I had missed an obvious point. "If you leave a food out, like an apple or a piece of bread, it goes mouldy in no time. Always. And you know why that is?"

I shook my head.

"It gets covered in spores and microbes because there's millions and millions of them floating in the air. The earth is the same—like an apple spinning in space. And there's all these germs landing on it and infecting it. From those millions and billions of stars himself was going on about."

"Microbes inside meteorites?" I said.

"Like a nutshell, to protect them from harmful radiations and so forth. All sorts of them, landing and infecting the earth all the time." His fingers mimed the falling of snowflakes "They land here, and they start growing. Tiny little seeds or mushroom spores or maggot eggs. And if they're not stamped out, they grow—sea monsters... and abominable snowmen... and other *things*."

Like tardigrades, I thought, remembering the little crawling creatures I had seen through Dr Evans's microscope. She said those little creatures could fold themselves up and hibernate and survive the rigours of space travel. That was how they spread out through the universe—not on rocket ships like the heroic explorers in science fiction, but as particles drifting through space like dandelion seed.

"And this one here, it's like a disease that infects everything. Only it's not a disease exactly; it's a 'different arrangement of matter.' Imbued with an energy alien to our planet and incompatible with our form of life."

I knew Skinner well enough to tell if he was putting me on, but he seemed utterly convinced by the explanation he had been given, even if perhaps he had not understood it as well as he thought. He sounded like a religious convert with words and phrases indelibly imprinted in his brain. Miss De Vere's powers of persuasion were greater than I had realised.

"And it's only Miss De Vere's people who fight the infection," he went on, as if picking her name from my mind. "They find it, and they sterilise it before the whole planet goes rotten."

"That's the government's job."

Skinner made a noise that might have been "Pshaw!" He never was taken with the government's way of doing things, not since the war.

"Any government that gets hold of something like this, they'll try and turn it into a new poison gas or germ warfare so they could destroy more cities. That's why she wants to get rid of it—so nobody finds out how to use it."

"So she says," I said.

"It's true." Skinner's eyes were wide. "They're defending the human race. It's got to be a better cause than Lord Wotsit. He only wants to get the Holy Grail for himself. You don't see him going to tell the government—or getting a proper doctor for that poor beggar with his fingers dropping off."

He had a point inasmuch as our patron was not behaving any better. Skinner knew that ideology was my weak spot, and he pressed his point. He had never shown any concern for Pierce before.

"It's dangerous stuff—playing with fire. You've seen that with your own two eyes. And that was just a tiny little piece of the baetyl. Now, I can't say whether it might not turn London into a desert, and neither can you. And you want to hand it over to him?"

I had no ready answer for that.

"Not that there's much prospect of us finding anything, is there?" he asked. "We don't have to fight over what we don't have."

"I am pursuing a lead."

"Good man!" Skinner punched me on the shoulder. "Once we find it, we'll have a few pints, and I'll prove the case to you properly, point by point. Can we declare a ceasefire until then?"

"Certainly," I said. Not that I trusted Skinner, who was always warning me not to trust anyone, least of all him, but unless we worked together, there was little prospect of success. And perhaps he did have a case. Stafford did not inspire trust. Although Miss De Vere did not seem any more trustworthy.

"What have you found?"

In truth, the credit all belonged to Hoade, but I preferred not to mention him to Skinner, who was always so secretive about business matters. The librarian had ferreted out a link between the Horniman Museum and the occult. The connection was a man called Samuel Mathers, one of the founders of the Hermetic Order of the Golden Dawn, a famous society of magical scholars that still exists to this day. Mathers was a polyglot who translated important texts with titles like *The Lesser Key of Solomon* and *The Grimoire of Armadel* from obscure ancient languages. He was a friend of W. B. Yeats, another member of the Golden Dawn, and the two had exchanged much intelligence on occult matters.

"But what's the connection?" Skinner asked.

"In 1890, Samuel Mathers, being strapped for cash, took up a new post in South London. Yeats mentions that Mathers lived on the edge of a big garden belonging to an eccentric rich man and arranged and dusted his curios."

I paused, and Skinner's eyes narrowed as the penny dropped.

"Horniman?"

"Horniman," I affirmed. "Mathers wasn't the actual curator—he was more a sort of janitor—but he had the run of it. If there was an important occult item hidden away in the collection—such as a baetyl, for example—he would surely have been the one to find it."

"That's a lead right enough," said Skinner. "Good work, Harry. How do we find this Mathers fellow?"

"Unfortunately, there is a difficulty there. He died in Paris in '18 during the Spanish-flu epidemic."

"Well, that's no good." Skinner slumped over in a parody of misery, chin on the table, and looked up at me. "What do we do now?"

"Mathers left a great many writings on the occult. If he found something important in the museum, he must mention it somewhere in one of his books even if only parenthetically. I'm going through the most promising chapters, but it's all rather…" I struggled for a word. "Rather opaque than otherwise."

Skinner eyed the pile of thick, square books at my elbow. Anything deeper than the *Daily Sketch* was too dense for his taste.

"Wait a minute," he said. "Are you telling me Mabel Brown read through all that lot?"

"She only had to come across the relevant passage in one book."

"You saw what her taste in reading matter was. Romantic and literary. More likely she was intimate with Mathers. There was a few scandals with that lot and young girls, weren't there?"

I did a mental calculation. If Mabel Brown was the same age as Elsie Granger, then she would have been about thirteen when Mathers died—and she would have had to have been in France. An intimacy with Mathers hardly seemed likely. She must have found the clue after he died, although I had to agree that none of his works fit in well with her interests.

"I'm trying the indexes first." I had been going through them all, looking for *baetyl, bethel, meteorite, aerolite, shooting star* and a few others. I had learned something at least from Hoade, not that it was doing me any good.

"Well, you keep up the good work here," Skinner said. "I'll find out what's happened to that cup of tea I asked for. And maybe I'll go out and get us some buns. I'm getting hungry now."

The rift between us had not exactly been healed, but it was papered over for the time being. As long as we had our common goal, we would be a team.

On his return, bearing the tea tray himself along with a heap of penny buns, Skinner finally opened the letter that had arrived in the early post. "Another summons to the manor house. At least it's not that lunatic gardener this time."

He passed me the note:

The Gipsy woman I mentioned will visit the Firs this afternoon, leaving the house between two and three. Follow her at a safe distance, on no account allowing yourselves to be seen. Maintain a record of her movements, keep a record of everyone she sees, and find out exactly where she is staying. If it is an encampment, we will need to know where within the encampment.

She claims she makes the water by harvesting the dew by starlight when it is exposed to certain arrangements of constellations. Look for any evidence of such activity but also any distillation apparatus or stores of unusual liquid or other possible sources.

Report back to me when you have her location. THIS IS VERY IMPORTANT.

"I believe Paracelsus mentions collecting dew," I said.

"It's a blind. Collecting dew is a bit of old gipsy palaver, what they say when they want to put you off the scent. And you don't want to trust Paracelsus. He put all sorts of japes into his recipes to stop the wrong sort of people copying him."

"Really?"

"Oh, yes," Skinner said as if it was common knowledge. "Any luck with Mathers?"

What I had discovered about Mathers was less than encouraging. He was, it was true, a founding member of the Golden Dawn, an organisation set up at the same time as, and in opposition to, Madame Blavatsky's Theosophists. I had come across one of the remnants of that group during the Roslyn D'Onston affair. The Golden Dawn had also fragmented, splitting into a multitude of hostile groups. Occultists were a fractious lot.

The Theosophists and Golden Dawn were not enemies but rivals. W. B. Yeats, perhaps thanks to his Irish charm, had succeeded in belonging to both. The Golden Dawn was largely given over to psychic experimentation of the sort that Miss De Vere would have deplored. They sought to project their consciousness across the gulfs of space to explore distant planets. Mathers, wielding a wooden mace, would trace out a mystic sequence of numbers on a tablet, and the viewers would be transported.

The worlds they discovered were suspiciously like romantic versions of our own. I have had cause to read up a little about the solar system, and I know something about the conditions on other planets. Mathers's description of Mars, with its vineyards and warring medieval principalities, seemed just as fictional as Edgar Rice Burroughs's Barsoom and a good deal less entertaining. Scientists are now in agreement that Mars is a dead world, freezing cold and almost airless. If there are any Martians, they are utterly alien beings.

The more I read about Mathers, the less I took to him. He changed his name from plain Mathers to MacGregor Mathers and called himself Comte de Glenstrae after a Jacobite he imagined was an ancestor. He was dictatorial and unbending to his fellow members of the Golden Dawn and insisted that he alone was in psychic contact with powerful, unseen beings. That form of communication conveniently allowed for no verification by anyone else and no means of challenging his pronouncements. He invited Aleister Crowley into the order and gave him a high rank, which caused much of the later trouble. By every account, Crowley was an evil man, perhaps as bad in his way as Roslyn D'Onston.

In later life, Mathers became increasingly eccentric and obsessed with the Jacobite cause. He took to walking the streets of Paris in full highland rig, including a kilt and several daggers. He claimed to be in psychic contact with the pretender to the throne of Scotland, planned to put him into power, and picked fights with anyone who questioned him. In addition, he seemed to think he was the earthly incarnation of the Egyptian god Osiris. It was rumoured he had tried to resurrect one of the Egyptian mummies at the Horniman cases, which made me think of palingenesis, but the experiment had evidently failed.

W. B. Yeats called him "half a lunatic, half knave," which was not a recommendation.

Mathers seemed like a victim of his own imagination. The Golden Dawn's exercises in projection sounded not unlike ordinary daydreaming to me, the main difference being that they were conducted at greater length and with a great deal of solemn ritual.

In short, he did not seem to be a man who could be relied upon. If he had discovered anything valuable while sorting through the accumulated dust heaps of Horniman's storage rooms, in between the mummy cases and the boxes of butterflies and the African idols, Mathers would surely have made something of it. But if his occult talent was, as I suspected, nothing more than showmanship, then Mathers lacked the skill to recognise an otherworldly specimen such as the baetyl.

Skinner summoned a taxi and ordered the driver to park around the corner from the big house and wait, keeping the meter running. The two of us then sauntered down the street. It was a broad avenue of expansive villas and not the sort of place where you could idle, but we found a shady tree where two men might pause and shelter from the afternoon sun, and we took advantage of it. Skinner's case, which was mainly to make us look more like commercial travellers, proved to contain greaseproof paper bags with an assortment of pork pies, scotch eggs, and some sausage rolls, which he had acquired from the baker that morning.

We made a picnic of it. I dare say a lot of others found excuses to do the same that day.

"An army marches on its stomach," Skinner observed placidly.

The view up and down the street also helped us reassure ourselves that we were not being followed in turn. Taking a taxicab was a good way of losing pursuers who were on foot or might be able to take a bus or tram.

At twenty past two, the gates of the Firs opened, and a small, round woman appeared. As luck would have it, she turned towards us and passed on the other side of the street. Skinner and I pretended to be deep in conversation.

The woman looked very much the gipsy in an ankle-length dress of rich red-and-blue material, her hair covered by a headscarf in contrasting shades. Instead of a handbag, she carried a wicker basket. She moved with the steady but determined pace of a beetle, her toes appearing with every forward step. She did not glance around at us but was occupied with her own thoughts. As she passed, I caught a flash of gold from her hands, which had rings on every finger.

We waited until she was almost at the end of the street before unhurriedly polishing off the last of our snacks, brushing off the crumbs, and making our way after her. She was a slow walker, and keeping up would be no trouble.

The pursuit was carried out in stages. Skinner was in the lead, and at intervals, I was sent back to the taxicab to instruct the driver where he should move to next. We had to make sure he was ready to hand in case we needed a conveyance, but a car could not park everywhere. As the afternoon wore on, we began to accept that the gipsy woman went everywhere on foot and that the taxi was an encumbrance as well as an extravagance.

She made first for Central Hill and spent some time going in and out of shops, principally those selling clothing but also an ironmonger. She met two women, who were evidently acquaintances, on the street and chatted a while with them. Then she made her way towards Sydenham Hill, where she paid a visit to a house situated on its own in the shadow of the wood: old Whatley's place. I knew him mainly by reputation; previously, when I had visited with Mr Yang, Whatley's daughter had refused to open the door to me.

The gipsy woman was admitted at once. We waited at a safe distance, leaning on a fence. Skinner picked a long piece of grass and chewed on it. Metallic green flies buzzed about, sometimes landing on the vegetation and moving with abrupt, mechanical bursts of speed. Higher up, hoverflies caught the sun as they slowly circled each other in a lazy dance. Investigations often involved a lot of hanging around and waiting. There were worse ways of spending a summer day.

"There used to be a big gipsy camp near here, at Gipsy Hill," Skinner told me as we leaned against a shady wall. "They were there for centuries. Maybe that's what brings her back."

"What happened to the camp?"

"The authorities started cracking down on them. But some say that masked men with torches came and burned them out."

Half an hour later, the gipsy woman emerged again, and we glimpsed Whatley's daughter in the doorway. The gipsy was carrying the same basket as before, and the weight of it had not changed much. She continued on foot at her slow, steady pace, and we followed at a decent interval.

We trailed her to a lane by the woods where a painted wooden caravan with enormous spoked wheels nestled under the trees. There was no sign of a horse, and judging from the grass growing around it, I did not think the caravan could have moved in the last two weeks.

Two dogs of the undifferentiated terrier variety were tied up outside. Her approach prompted excited barking and tail wagging. She mounted the wooden stair and let herself into the caravan with a key.

"And that is all about that," said Skinner, not without satisfaction. "Stand easy, Bombardier. Our objective has been obtained. With no casualties."

A minute later, the caravan door opened, and the woman came out with a bowl of scraps for the dogs. She proceeded to sit on the step and talk to the animals while she peeled potatoes.

"I thought gipsies camped together," I said.

"It's because she's a *choveck,*" he said tightly. "A witch. They have to stay apart from the rest. The clean don't mix with the unclean."

Skinner knew something of gypsies from his carnival days. I would have stayed and watched for longer, but he was for moving on. "She's settled in for a bit now. I intend to take up a strategic position in the Bird in Hand public house and relay a report of the day's action to headquarters while refuelling the unit's engines. Come on, before she sees you gawping."

I was reluctant and suggested that one of us should remain to keep an eye on the caravan in case she went out again. Skinner noted that she had changed her shoes for slippers and showed every sign of being finished for the day. At that point, we heard voices; some men were approaching. We turned around as three men rounded the curve of the path.

They were labourers in canvas trousers and wool shirts

with leather waistcoats and hats. Their colourful kerchiefs and dark complexions suggested they were at least part gipsy if not full-blooded Romanies. One of them carried a long instrument over his shoulder, something like a scythe, and the other two had shorter sickles.

They stopped when they saw us.

"What're you doing here?" demanded the first, an older man with a long moustache and a gold ring through one ear.

It was a fair question. From our location, anyone might have reasonably suspected that we were spying on the caravan and its occupant.

The man with the scythe and the one with the sickle placed their feet farther apart and changed the way they were holding their tools. I had seen gipsies in the ring many times and even fought against a gipsy myself on one occasion. I had a healthy respect for them. Generalisations could be dangerous. Most boxers might be Jewish, but not everyone who spoke Hebrew could punch like Kid Lewis or even Sammy Gold; plenty of them were as weedy as any Anglo-Saxon. But the gipsies had always been a great race for boxing and still quite dominated the field when it came to the bare-knuckle sport. They were great fighters—tough as nails and fast as lightning. As a rule, their boxing style was uneducated but not unskilful, and could wear down a boxer with greater technical knowledge if he did not keep his wits about him. They took punishment and kept taking it in a way that few others could match.

I judged the layout of the situation like a geometric puzzle. If I left the lead man to Skinner, I would have to move fast to take on the other two. Surely, they would not use deadly force, and a scythe made a clumsy weapon. Still, if the bearer was sufficiently angered he might use it—

In the fraction of a second I had been calculating the odds for a fight, Skinner had already started speaking. "Gentlemen! We're looking for Mr Whatley's residence. We were thinking of asking the lady in the caravan, but we did not wish to alarm her. Do you know Mr Whatley by any chance, I believe he's friendly with the *Zingari* people?"

"Can't help you, pal."

The last word was said quite disrespectfully. That we were wearing suits cut no ice with these gentlemen. That Skinner knew some of their language made them suspicious.

"Perhaps you could pause and think a second." Skinner spun a silver sixpence in the air. "Just in case anything comes to you. Perhaps you don't know the name Whatley, but he lives in a cottage down one of these lanes, and there are not many of those… but we seem to have been misdirected. We're not bailiff's men or anything, are we?"

"No, we're not bailiff's men," I echoed when Skinner looked up at me. Caught off guard, I said it so woodenly and with such lack of conviction that nobody hearing it would have been convinced.

"Not bailiff's men?" repeated the moustachioed man, eyes on the spinning coin. "Well… you could try going down there and taking the next lane on the left about a quarter mile."

I noted that he did not admit to knowing Whatley or even of having seen any cottages in the area. It was a well-crafted reply, one that a lawyer might have admired. I noted also that he was sending us in the wrong direction for Whatley.

"We'll give that a try, then," said Skinner with a smile, tossing the coin to him. The gipsy caught it one-handed as easily as a lizard caught a fly with its tongue.

"Thank you very much for your assistance, gentlemen," said Skinner, touching the brim of his hat.

"Much obliged," I added with the same gesture.

"Afternoon," said the gipsy, no friendlier than before, but the three of them parted to let us pass.

I was still wary that they might assault us, and the back of my neck prickled, but as soon as we were past, they carried on their way. We heard them call out a greeting to the woman in the caravan, and I saw them doffing their hats and bowing most politely, even reverently.

On Skinner's insistence, we repaired to the pub, where he stood me a pint. The place was busy, and no wonder on such a hot day. A cool beer could not have been more welcome.

"You know what nearly happened there?" said Skinner after the ritual of the first swallow and a long pause to appreciate it.

"What?"

"We could have been mowed down!" He seemed more pleased by his own word play than concerned about the encounter.

"It was close enough."

"They're as suspicious of us *gajoes*—outsiders—as we are of them," said Skinner. "They must be here for the fair. It's like a rendezvous point when you're all wanderers with no fixed abode."

"It must be a strange life."

"It has its charms," Skinner agreed, then suddenly his mood dipped. His squib about being mowed down had brought back memories. "And Christ, all those poor bastards not here to enjoy it, lying under the sod in Flanders Field." He took a long pull of his beer. "It's up to us to drink the pints they can't drink and make love to the women they'll never know. To feel the sun…" There was a choke in his voice.

"It's not your fault. It was the war."

"I led them over the top," he said. "'Come on, lads. Last one to the wire is a sissy…' They trusted me. They should never have trusted me! And somehow, the bullets always missed me so I could do it again and again."

I wanted to explain that those men would have died whatever Skinner had done, that the whole thing was out of the hands of men like us. There was something bigger at work that was as inevitable as the seasons. The whole giant machinery of it had been set in motion years before, and it would grind up millions more, whatever happened. I did not know how that machinery was built or why, I just knew that it was there. But I did not have the words to express myself.

"It was a bad business," I said. "You were just doing your bit."

"Thanks, Harry." He patted my arm and took another drink.

I was thinking about a different war—the one that Miss De Vere and her friends were fighting—and the wasteland of the future she had shown me. Skinner and I were in battle again, and we hardly knew which side we were on.

Chapter Thirteen

Reading the Leaves

I am not, as you may have gathered, a great one for deception or subterfuge. My acting skills are rudimentary. Hence, I prefer the straightforward approach where possible. I like to state my business plainly and deal like an honest man. But as both Skinner and my correspondence course have advised me, this is not always fruitful in the investigation business, and more often than not, an oblique angle is advisable.

Even so, I had misgivings as I approached the gipsy caravan with Sally by my side, knowing that we were going under false pretences. It was a pleasant summer evening, balmy enough for me to go jacketless. The air smelled of fresh-cut grass and honeysuckle, the blackbirds were singing, but I was apprehensive.

Apart from anything else, I recalled that Sir Ernest Shackleton had been told by a gipsy that he would die at the age of forty-eight. He had dropped dead in exactly that year even though he had seemed strong as an ox and was leading an expedition to the Antarctic. I did not believe in fortune tellers, even gipsy ones, but I should not wish to hear my fate pronounced like that.

And Skinner, usually so keen to walk into the lion's jaws, had been spooked by the very idea of talking to the woman. He was not a superstitious man, but he did not like the idea of meeting her face-to-face one bit, though he would not explain why he was afraid. I suspected the fear had rubbed off on him from the gipsies he had known who'd made a sign to ward off the evil eye whenever something unlucky was mentioned. That sort of thing was contagious.

"Don't worry," Sally said, taking my arm. "I'll do all the talking. You just keep your eyes open and look out for whatever it is you're looking out for."

The gipsy woman was sitting on the back step of the caravan, with a basket of sewing, under a sort of portico behind the front door. The dogs lifted their heads in unison, uncertain whether to bark.

"Hello," said Sally brightly. "I'm Sally. You remember my note? I said around seven o'clock. I hope you were expecting us."

"One time's as good as another for me," said the gipsy, putting her work aside.

"This is Harry."

I nodded and removed my bowler.

"Pleased, I'm sure. You can call me Madam Hester."

Up close, the caravan's decorations proved to be highly elaborate. It was not just painted, but every panel was a different picture, making a whole parade of images, and the supports between were covered in gold leaf filigreed to a remarkable level of detail. The whole thing was as neat as a pin.

"Your caravan is quite a work of art." I let the dogs sniff my hand. They wagged their tails energetically and licked my fingers. They seemed like friendly beasts.

"Do they bite?" asked Sally.

"Wouldn't be much use as guard dogs if they didn't," said the gipsy. "I suppose you two had better come in."

She rose to her feet and opened the door behind her. We went up the steep wooden steps after her and into the interior of the caravan.

I reached the top step and looked into the shadowy interior. "Should I remove my shoes?"

"No, no, just come in." She was lighting a candle. "But before we start, it's two shillings. Each."

She laughed at Sally's horror. Four shillings was a day's pay in the pickle factory.

"I've got grandchildren and grandnieces and grandnephews.

There's no work, and gipsies don't live on fresh air and sunshine," she said. "Besides, the more you pay, the more you'll listen. Four shillings, and you'll pay the proper attention."

I handed over the money without demur. Hester secreted the coins in a hidden pocket.

"Whose idea was it to come to me?"

"Hers," I said, and Hester gave a knowing smile, as though she already had the measure of us.

The interior of the caravan was more spacious than I expected, the barrel-vaulted roof giving a good clearance even for one of my height. The layout was much like that of a small boat, with all the conveniences of everyday life reproduced in compact form and everything tidily stowed away. There was a stove built in to one side, a curtained alcove that had to be a bunk, and two separate washbasins. No books anywhere, though. Many gipsies, especially the older ones, were as averse to reading as Skinner. The interior was quite as ornate as the exterior; almost every surface was decorated with the most intricate woodcarvings, including the curved ceiling.

After a time, I saw that some of the carvings were of a disquieting nature, with little details that made them monstrous. I was especially struck by a carving on a pillar that showed trees with hands and twisted faces and roots coiling like serpents. Why would someone choose to live with such decoration? Lit by one candle, the caravan felt like a deep cave, the retreat of some obscure and sinister cult. Perhaps it was only menacing to outsiders.

Hester directed us to sit on a sort of padded chest, which made a comfortable and sturdy seat. After a moment, she passed us two steaming cups. Up close, I could see that her face was a mass of fine wrinkles, though her hair was jet black and I would have been hard put to guess her age. She had reached a point where the passage of years would no longer alter her appearance.

"Now then, my dear. Why don't you tell me all about it?" Hester said.

"We want to get married," said Sally hesitantly, looking at me and back to the gipsy. "But there is a difficulty."

"Ah, there always is, my dear. There always is. It's your past, isn't it?"

Sally almost dropped the teacup in surprise.

"How did you know…?"

"It's my business to know—ain't that why you came here?" She laughed, and there was an edge to that laugh I did not like. "I'm sorry, my dear. Do go on, now."

Madam Hester was shrewd, but I'd read enough Sherlock Holmes stories to know she did not need to employ psychic powers to make such a deduction. The mark left by an old wedding ring, people's shoes and clothing, and the calluses on their hands were all marks that could be read by someone who knew how. And a person might be able to guess a few things from seeing a couple our age, after the first flush of youth, dressed as we were.

"We haven't been together very long," said Sally, and that was true enough. She'd made the suggestion that we present ourselves as a courting couple only a few hours previously. As Sally had pointed out, women quite often went to gipsies to have fortunes told, whereas men almost never did. The only way for me to get into the caravan was in the company of a woman, and the plan had more or less hatched itself from that point onwards.

Sally was telling Hester about her first husband and the child. Hester was watching her closely, taking it all in, and that gave me an opportunity to surreptitiously inspect the caravan.

My first objective was to assess the potentialities for effecting an entrance. I had examined the lock on the back door on the way in. I now inspected the window fastenings, the hatch on one side, and the small front door.

I also attempted to locate all the places we would need to take account of if we wanted to carry out a search. But every vertical surface seemed to be a cupboard door or a drawer, and every horizontal surface seemed to be the top of a chest. The maximum amount of stowage had been incorporated into the fabric of the caravan. The thing was a masterpiece of design and contained as many potential hiding places as a decent-sized house.

And there were the dogs to consider as well.

"I was on my own. No money. Debts piling up and a baby to look after," Sally was saying. There was a catch in her voice. "I only had one thing I could sell. Lots of women do it."

"There, there," said Hester. "That's all over now."

"Harry's family don't know anything about it."

"No—and what have you told them about Sally?" Hester asked, turning to me.

"Not a thing. They don't know about her at all," I said. "They might have an idea I'm seeing someone."

"Harry saved me," said Sally quietly. "He believed in me when nobody else did."

I shrugged modestly at this embroidering of the truth. It began to occur to me that Sally might not be entirely acting and that my part in the subsequent events and the final defeat of Roslyn D'Onston really had made me a hero in her eyes.

Hester nodded sagely. "Finish your tea now. Just leave a dreg in the bottom, and we'll see what the leaves have to say."

Sally passed her cup over. Hester swirled it around three times, poured the tea into a saucer, and inspected the tea leaves that remained in the cup. The rings on her fingers gleamed in the candlelight as she turned the cup to inspect its contents.

I watched closely to see what she was doing and was reminded irresistibly of Mr Yang's curious oriental divination practices. Some of those were probably empty rituals, but he did have the ability to uncover information that was not accessible to normal human senses.

"The bottom of the cup is the past, the sides are the present, and nearest the rim is what's to come," she said. "We have to look at the patterns the tea leaves make, that's the art. Now, my dear, in your past I see a man and the letter *C*."

"Eddie Collins," said Sally. "He's not coming back, is he?" Collins was the man who had made money off of Sally when she was on the streets. She'd paid for his "protection."

"No, he's gone for good," Hester said. I wondered how she could speak with such quiet confidence. Collins had last been seen heading to Manchester, but it was possible that he would show up again and want to take up where he had left off. "He's only in your past. In your present I see a veil—that means secrets—and an anvil, which means hard work and effort."

She paused, and again Sally filled in the gaps for her.

"They're telling the truth there. Factory work is no picnic; that's for sure."

"And in your future… there are clouds. That means changes and challenges. And a chain; that can mean captivity or something else…"

I wondered if she was hinting at matrimony, but before Sally could enquire further, Hester put her cup down and took up mine.

"And what do we have here?" She looked from me to the cup. "In your past—a candle, which means trials and worries. Fighting and violence."

"I've had my share," I said, unimpressed. Anyone who saw me might have made a similar speculation.

"A comet—that's an unexpected visitor from far away."

My jaw might have dropped open at that point.

"See—it's right here in the cup." She pointed out a blob of leaves that was more of a comma or a tadpole than a comet. "And a corkscrew, which means your curiosity sometimes gets you into trouble." She gave me a sly look. "Is that right, Harry?"

"Sometimes," said Sally.

"And in the future—a beetle."

That made my scalp prickle sure enough. I was ready to believe that she really was a witch.

"In the language of tea leaves, a beetle means a difficult undertaking—or a scandal." She glanced at Sally. "And a lamp, which can mean help from others or the uncovering of secrets."

"Anything else?" asked Sally, hoping perhaps for some sign of a wedding.

"A man, a winged man—but he's farther off. But I see a woman," said Hester slowly. "Another woman."

The silence in the caravan grew.

"My mother?" I hazarded.

"No," said Sally. "It's *her*."

"I can't see her clearly. Why is that, hey?" Madam Hester looked up sharply as though it was her fault. "Is she your rival?"

Both women looked at me.

"She's a rich woman who wants me to work for her," I said. "But she means well, I think."

"Can you tell anything else about her?" asked Sally. "Her name is Estelle De Vere, and she comes from America."

"She'll come between you if you let her." Hester turned the cup this way and that as though trying to make Miss De Vere's image come clearer through the leaves. "And round her… like burning flames maybe… what does that mean?" For the first time, she seemed puzzled, almost alarmed. "No, I don't like the look of her."

"I don't like her either," said Sally.

"She's an obstacle," said Hester. "A danger."

"What should we do?"

"The leaves don't say," said Hester, putting the cup down. "They never tell you yea or nay. That's not the way of it. They just show you where you are. Give you something to think about."

She looked at us speculatively. Human life was an old, old story to her. She was shrewd enough to see through the deceit on both sides that all too often preceded a wedding—the falsehoods and empty promises that men and women both used to secure a mate. She had seen so many anxious querents asking about their prospective husbands and the doubts they harboured. She had seen the whole sorry round of disappointments, infidelities, and crashes into poverty. I suppose she had lost some human sympathy in the process.

Madam Hester had the air of a doctor who was only interested in patients with spectacularly unusual conditions and was resigned to let the normal course of mortality overtake the others. Sally and I were, perhaps, an unusual case.

"Do you ever look at your own future?" Sally asked.

"Lord, no," said Hester. "It's something we only do for… the natives of the land. But I can see things others can't." She raised her voice. "Like when a spy wants to sneak in and steal my secrets."

Her gaze was cold steel, stabbing into my eyeballs like a stiletto, and I drew my breath. She possessed that lethal power known as the evil eye, which could paralyse the strongest man.

"I'm not scared of you," she said, or rather sneered, as I managed to look away.

"I should hope not," I said. "I've never made a habit of intimidating women, and don't plan to start. You've no cause to fear me. I'm on a mission of mercy."

That gave Madam Hester pause. She had been ready to deliver a speech about spies and sneaks, perhaps had been looking forward to it, but the line of discussion had been diverted.

"There's this man," I said, "an acquaintance, who has been suffering from something, and the doctors don't know what it is."

"What's that to me?"

"His mind has gone, and his body is withering away. His skin is as white and dusty as chalk."

That took her by surprise too, but after a second, she cackled. It was an ugly laugh, and she carried on for longer than was needful as though she found the news genuinely funny.

"Nobody can save men from their own folly," she said at last. "That's beyond my powers, or anyone's. But don't you worry; your friend won't die. No, he won't *die*."

"This thing," I said. "It's dangerous, and I have reason to believe it might spread."

"Of course it's *dangerous*," she said mockingly. "That's why it has to be kept secret. And if it spreads, so much the worse!"

She cackled again, even more mirthfully than before, but when she had finished, her face was stern.

"Please, madam—"

"You're not getting my secrets! Now, you two, get out of my home. You've had what you paid for." She waved a hand. "Go. Go and get married if you think it'll do you any good."

I tried to apologise, but she shooed us out. "Go, go."

I negotiated the wooden steps with slight difficulty in the dark and helped Sally down after me. One of the dogs gave a small "wuff" as we passed, and then he was silent.

"Well, you had to try," said Sally. "Did you see anything?"

"Not much. I don't think there's anything there to see."

"At least we did get our fortunes told." She turned to me, all serious. "Do you think she really can see the future?"

"Maybe she sees something sometimes, but mainly, she's a shrewd guesser," I said. "I bet she knows all the ins and outs of love affairs and what people are really thinking."

"I wouldn't go back there. That laugh made me shiver."

"You did a good job of keeping her talking."

The lane was quiet; there was not another soul about.

"I was scared when she looked in the tea leaves," she said, taking my arm in agitation. "I was worried she was going to say something about my boy. I kept thinking of that story, the one where a man goes to a fortune teller, and the gipsy looks at his hand and straightway gives him his money back and refuses to tell him anything. The man keeps asking him, but the gipsy gets angry and turns him out. And as soon as he goes onto the street, he gets run over by a bus and killed." She laughed. "It's only a silly story..."

"Stories about fortune tellers are always like that," I said. "The message is always, 'No good can come of this.' Whoever circulates these stories wants to discourage people from ever trying the experiment."

"Why does she do it? Fortune telling, I mean. D'you think it's because she likes prying into other folks' lives?"

"That and the money," I said. "Though as to that... I was reading about witchcraft, and one of the old witch finders said the powers the devil gave witches were all a delusion. Otherwise, they wouldn't all be ugly old crones living in hovels—they'd make themselves young and beautiful and rich."

The night sky was velvety black, but the more I looked, the more tiny blue-white points of light appeared. Still tinier stars emerged in the gaps between. Stafford would surely be able to count his five thousand stars with his telescope that night.

"Let's sit down a bit," Sally said as we reached a bench. "I wouldn't sit out in the dark, but it's such a warm night. And I feel safe with you. You're so strong."

"You're a game girl, Sally. I don't believe that this enterprise, harmless as it may seem, is at all free from risk."

"Mr Skinner seemed to think it was all a lark."

"Skinner has a want of seriousness," I said then relented. "If you take his pronouncements at face value."

"Life's too serious to take too seriously." It was a quote from musical comedy and usually said flippantly, but Sally said it so wistfully that I had an uncomfortable glimpse of the life behind her.

People needed a bit of something cheerful to see them through, especially if they were working long hours in a pickle factory. I had my friends in Conquering Hero and at the gymnasium, and I had Sunday lunch with the whole family to look forward to. Sally had no family and no friends from her previous life except perhaps among the nuns at Virgo Fidelis, and she ached for missing her son.

A bat fluttered overhead, swooping this way and that. I was about to point it out when Sally suddenly spoke up. "Harry, did you ever think about what life would be like if you were married?"

"I can't say that I have."

"In a few years, wouldn't you like to live in your own place rather than someone else's? Have someone to cook properly for you and keep company with?" She spoke dreamily. "Maybe some little ones, one day?"

"I suppose it's what everyone wants." My rented room was in fact beginning to feel cramped; it was not having anywhere to put books that did it. I supposed I could get something larger than a room, but that would mean a housekeeper, and the complications that entailed had put me off the idea.

As for women and courting and marriage, those were worlds apart for me. I could not imagine how it would ever come about that I would be in a position to propose, given all the steps in between. How would I even meet a woman?

"I know you're not comfortable around any women," Sally said, reading my mind. "But you could do a lot worse."

I abruptly realised that she was still holding my arm; she was talking about my marrying her.

"I know," she said, although I had not said anything. "I have a past. God knows I have a past. But we've got shared history, you and me. You can talk to me like you can't talk to anyone else about things. And I *understand.* About beetles and things."

That was true. Sally knew more about my work than even my family. She had seen things that no other living human had seen.

"I don't want charity," she went on. "I've had enough of that from the nuns. With you and me, it'll be a real partnership, fifty-fifty. I can cook and clean and keep house and everything… and you can trust me. With everything."

"Is that a shooting star?"

"Let's wish on it," she said.

But I saw at once that it was not a shooting star. The fierce red glow that drifted above us, in among the placid blue-white stars, went for too long before going out. Then another and another went by. We both gawped upward and followed the stream of glowing embers back to their source: an angry red glow from behind the trees, just in the direction that we had come from.

I hurried back, and as I approached, I could hear the dogs barking at the wooden caravan, whose gaily painted sides were burning like a funeral pyre, wrapped in long ribbons of red-yellow flame that twisted round each other. The fire roared like a blast furnace and, even as I watched it, the caravan started collapsing in on itself. The intensity was astonishing as though the caravan had been dipped in paraffin before being set alight.

"Hester!" I called.

There was no sign of her, and the caravan door was still shut. She could hardly have fallen asleep in that time. There had been no fire burning when we had left. Even if she had lit the stove for a brew, I could not see how it could have run out of control so fast.

"Hester!"

It would only be three steps to get out of the caravan, even if it was burning and she had stayed in too long trying to put the fire out, but somehow, I did not think Madame Hester had escaped.

The dogs barked furiously. Their chains were at full stretch, and they were barking into the fire.

Shadows bent around the trees two fields away. They were cast by a pair of car headlights, moving swiftly down the next lane.

Sally watched the holocaust wordlessly.

"Well, this is a right mess," I said.

Chapter Fourteen

A. E. F. Horniman

"Don't ever marry if you can help it," said Skinner. "That's my advice."

We were seated on a park bench, and he waited until a woman pushing a perambulator had passed before continuing.

"You don't have to marry her, I take it?"

"Of course not," I said. "Nothing could have been further from my mind."

"Well, there you are. Unfortunate about Madam Hester, though."

"*Unfortunate* hardly covers it."

"First Mabel Brown, then our second-hand dealer, and now your gipsy woman. His Gills will not be happy with another dead end. This here is our last and final chance."

I could not, of course, prove that Miss De Vere was behind the violent fire that had gutted the caravan in seconds. But the circumstantial evidence was considerable. Her aim of eliminating dangerous knowledge, and the fact that she had tabs on the two of us, argued for it. It also conveniently cast doubt on my own integrity, driving a wedge between Stafford and me—which was exactly what she wanted—while at the same time furnishing her with a piece of information she could use for blackmail. Both Skinner and Sally had urged me against informing the police that Sally and I had been the last people to see Madam Hester alive, and with some reluctance, I had kept my peace.

At least a new line of investigation had opened up. I had

been in the library on a dual quest. One half of it had been successful. On the matter of life travelling through space on meteoroids, there was quite a collection of literature, culminating with a Swedish chemist called Arrhenius, who thought that all life originated in that way and spread across the stars. There was even a word for it, *panspermia,* which I duly made note of. Perhaps a meteorite containing alien spores might really be a magna mater, a Great Mother to all kinds of troubling creatures.

However, the second part of my quest, looking through still-more-unlikely books by Mathers for possible revelations concerning his time as curator at the Horniman museum, was proving utterly fruitless.

In the midst of that, there was a polite cough at my elbow. "Ah, Stubbs," said Hoade, looking awkward and doing his best to hide behind his beard. "I didn't see you there earlier."

"Good morning, Hoade." I was always pleased to see him, as I knew he would not approach me unless he had some nugget of information to impart. Hoade was not the sort to say hello just for the sake of politeness.

"I'm sorry, Stubbs. I've been an ass," he said abruptly. "Mathers is a complete red herring."

"Why do you say that?"

"Because there's a far better and more obvious connection between the Golden Dawn and the Horniman Museum. I jumped at Mathers because he came out first and seemed to fit. You would have thought that cross-word puzzles had taught me not to use the first, obvious answer. But no." He shook his head sheepishly. "It's Annie Horniman."

"A member of the Horniman family?"

"Granddaughter of Honest John Horniman, who made the family fortune. Daughter of Frederick Horniman, who created the museum. She was the friend of Mathers who got him the post there. She was also a chum of Yeats, and she joined the Golden Dawn at the same time as him."

Hoade reasoned, sensibly enough, that Annie Horniman had more familiarity with the collection than Mathers, having lived with it in the same house for years. Given her interest in the occult, she was likely to have come across the baetyl. My researches on Mathers suggested that, while he might be good at translating old books, he was pretty impervious to ideas that were not his own, and Annie Horniman might be a better candidate.

Unlike the late Liddell Mathers, Miss Horniman was not only alive, but she was living in London—and able, we hoped, to answer a few questions. Of course, they would have to be put in the right way, and that was the trick. She was quite an important figure in theatrical circles. She had broken with the Golden Dawn and with Mathers and with W. B. Yeats, but her association with the latter included her setting up a theatre with him in Dublin. He had moved from magic to poetry, and she to theatre.

And Hoade, genius that he was, had found it child's play to locate Miss Horniman for me.

"I am greatly in your debt," I said.

"It's nothing," he said, sounding almost offended. "Oh, and another piece of minutiae, as you were asking—I can't find anything to link Pandora's box with meteorites except very indirectly. In fact, in the earliest versions of the myth, it was Pandora herself who was the bearer of trouble—she was created by the gods, the perfect woman, as a trap for mankind."

"How peculiar."

"Oh, not really," he said, glancing down at his wedding ring with a little smile.

"That reminds me—do not mention any of this to anyone. It's life or death. Especially," I added, "if there's a blond American lady asking."

"I won't. And I'll certainly watch out for American blondes."

He seemed unmoved, but somewhere behind those glasses, I suspected that there was a small thrill of vicarious adventure. I hoped that if Miss De Vere appeared, he would quell his impulse to share information and would stay silent. I did not want her knowing that he knew anything about baetyls or occult connections. A man who was in a position to learn more might qualify as a danger in her view.

It struck me that a library full of books was a dangerously

inflammable place and that all that dry paper only needed a match to set it off.

"If you're working here on your own after hours," I said, "try to keep a fire extinguisher handy."

The hall was beginning to fill up. The audience was largely female and of middle years, though there were some men among the older attendees. I was in my good suit, and Skinner had spruced himself up for the occasion. He smelled of eau de cologne and had his hair slicked back and a fresh flower in his buttonhole.

I felt more than usually out of place. The other folk were moneyed, but they were not exactly the smart set. They were more those types of middle-class, arty-crafty people who have a cultivated air of casualness. They were the sorts of people who filled the concert halls and galleries and attended educational public talks. They could tell the paintings of one artist from another and comment when the bassoon was off-key. They might not all have known each other personally, but they could recognise their own kind and those who were not of their own kind. The two of us attracted the odd curious glance. Or perhaps they were just looking at me.

The subject of the talk was the future of the theatre, a topic on which I was entirely ignorant and Skinner even more so.

"I don't see how they're going to fill five minutes with that," he grumbled, looking from the program to the rostrum, where the speakers were readying themselves, "never mind an hour."

The plan was that after the talk, Skinner would instigate a conversation with Miss Horniman, and he would develop the situation from there as needed. He harboured no doubts about his ability to establish a rapport with her; according to Skinner, he was able to engage any woman, even one from such a superior social class, as easily as a snake fascinated a rabbit.

"Even a wealthy, educated woman in her sixties?" I had asked him when he first floated the idea.

"Nothing to it," he said. "A little bit of flattery goes a long way with women that age—they're starved for it. Is that your homework you're working on?"

Now, while Skinner fidgeted, I was writing up my account of recent events, in which I had fallen somewhat behind. Even without what you might call a full-time job, it was surprising how few hours I had left in the day to catch up after taking into account my need to maintain a level of fitness at the gymnasium, my social obligations, and my correspondence course.

"Just trying to keep up to date on the 'insurance policy,'" I said.

The talk was a discussion with three participants: Miss A. E. F. Horniman, Mr K. N. Smith. and Dr W. Reese. Smith was an American gentleman from New York who smiled a great deal and found everyone charming. He was the referee, and he made introductory remarks and supplied the others with topics, not that they needed much to start them up.

The meat of the discussion was a battle between Miss Horniman and Dr Reese over whether the theatre was, in a manner of speaking, going to hell in a handbasket or whether it was in fact healthier than ever.

I did not recognise the names of any of the playwrights mentioned, or their works, and still less the directors or other parties involved. Comedy and "crook" plays, which were all I ever went to, were dismissed on all sides. A Russian called Tchechov was mentioned repeatedly. As for theatre business, I did not even know what a mushroom syndicate was or why it would be such a bad thing.

It was like one of those neighbourhood quarrels going back years, where old doings were raked over and misdemeanours taken out and aired and everyone understood what Joe had done to Bert.

Dr Reese was a literary man from Oxford, whose ruddy complexion indicated a familiarity with his college's wine cellars. He was unforgiving towards the modern world and the way that the vandals had made free with our theatrical heritage and besmirched—his word—our great treasures. The great dramas of human emotion had been replaced with cheap sensationalism and lewd displays that were unfit to put on the stage.

Miss Horniman listened to all that with great patience. She

was a plain woman with short-cropped grey hair and little sign of vanity about her person. Most women of that type sported turbans and gaudy brooches, but she was as unadorned as she was straight-talking.

When Miss Horniman spoke, it was with great conviction and a surprising flair. Art was not a mirror but a hammer; it needed to reshape the world and not just reflect it. For her, putting on a new play was about effecting social change and addressing the issues of the day, even if that included subjects that some people might consider sordid or unpleasant.

"Yes, we can have Shakespearean tragedies about the fall of kings, but let us not have *just* Shakespeare. Let us have works that the ordinary man—and the ordinary woman—can see, which chime with their own experience of the world. Theatre should not be dull and worthy, just for scholars. And pedants." She gave a sideways look at Dr Reese, which drew a laugh.

Miss Horniman recounted her experiences with productions in Dublin, Manchester, London, and Canada, and she contrasted the audiences. In her view, it was the job of the theatre to put on plays that people would want to watch. She recited a poem from memory by "Willie"—W. B. Yeats—about the frustration of dealing with knaves and dolts and theatre managers and how important it was that someone took on that task.

She was quite passionate in her speech and very convincing. Theatre sounded like an exciting, eye-opening, and important experience when she talked about it. I even thought I might go and see a play myself afterwards.

There were some long-winded questions from the audience afterwards. Skinner was yawning. I thought he would be getting ready to make his move, but he was rooted.

"You must be joking," he said sourly. "Look at her. She's even wearing trousers, for Gawd's sake. Her type isn't interested in men. We'll have to find an alternative line of attack because this one is a dead loss."

Miss Horniman was having an animated discussion with Mr Smith about costumes and scenery and the merits of a mobile production.

"Maybe I'll have a crack myself," I said, not meaning to speak out loud.

"You? Be my guest, Harry, but don't say I didn't warn you. I'll be waiting outside."

For some reason, smoking was not allowed in the lecture hall, and Skinner was panting for a cigarette. I let him go and gingerly made my way to the front of the room.

I was not at all certain how I would manage an introduction, given that Miss Horniman was at the centre of a knot of people. Only one of them was actively engaged with her—a stooped, balding man whose insistent tone carried over to where I was. Evidently, he was telling her about a theatre in Bristol, but as soon as she caught my eye, I distinctly heard her interrupt him midflow.

"You will have to excuse me, Mr Dean. I must just talk to a friend." She stepped over to me. "Delighted to meet you," she said, extending a hand. "Mr Dean is so tiresome. He knows he won't get another penny out of me for that folly of his in Bristol, but he will keep on about it every time he sees me. I'm not a bank."

"It's an honour, Miss Horniman," I said, taking her hand cautiously, though her grip was strong enough. "My name is Harry Stubbs, and I was very impressed with your talk, very impressed indeed. You beat that Reeves on points fair and square, three rounds to nothing."

"Thank you. Some men still entertain outdated ideas, and we need to put them right. You're not in the theatre business yourself?"

I had long since learned to accept that people made assumptions based on my appearance and my accent even when I was in my best suit. Perhaps I expected Miss Horniman to be more perceptive, and my disappointment, coupled with the excitement of the situation, spurred me to say more than I meant to.

"As a matter of fact, I'm a writer."

"Well, bully for you, Mr Stubbs," she said promptly. "As I was saying, Britain needs more playwrights with a true understanding of the average man."

"I'm really more of a novelist than a playwright at the present time." Lying has never been my talent, and I must have coloured like a schoolboy. To cover my embarrassment, I held up my sheaf of notes in evidence as though Miss Horniman might not believe otherwise that I really could string words together.

"Oh, a manuscript." To my surprise she took the top few sheets and, placing gold-rimmed half glasses on her nose, started reading. "I don't have much to do with novels. If you were to adapt it for the stage, I might be able to give you some names. It's a little old-fashioned in style."

"I dare say it is," I said.

"But is it a serious work?"

"I don't know if that's for me to say," I started but then decided to strike back rather than dodging. "If a work succeeds in reflecting life in a way that people can recognise, then it deserves to be taken seriously—even a modern work in a popular genre. The first job of any work is to be read. And if it distorts real life, then, like a lens, the distortion can be what magnifies."

Miss Horniman had said something similar in her talk, but she did not resent hearing her own argument. Far from it. She flipped pages. Unless she was an extraordinarily fast reader, she could only have been reading a few words from each.

"A gipsy fortune teller? That's a rather hackneyed device, if I may say so." She looked at me over her glasses.

"People still go to fortune tellers," I said. "And as a matter of fact, that was why I desired to talk to you—because you are an authority in matters relating to what is popularly called magic."

"Ah. Ah." I had surprised her but not for the reason I expected. "The cards never lie. I still use the Tarot from time to time, and it warned me to expect someone today." She gave me an appraising look as though I had just walked in. "The cards said I would meet a knight on a quest. That must be you."

"I wouldn't describe myself in those terms—"

"Excuse me, Miss Horniman," cut in a man with a notepad and a pen, touching her elbow. "I wonder if you could possibly—"

"Excuse *me,* Mr Collier," Miss Horniman snapped back. "I'll get to you quite soon enough when I've finished talking to Mr Stubbs."

Collier backed off with a sickly smile. This was it. We were getting to the do-or-die part of the conversation. I was still improvising furiously, but that often worked better for me than trying to think it all out beforehand. Sometimes you needed to trust your reflexes.

"This is about the Golden Dawn, isn't it?" she asked. "And those beastly experiments. The reason I left."

"I wasn't aware of the background to your leaving."

"The reason I left," she said levelly, "was over the idea that there should be marital relations between an elemental spirit and a human woman. My views on the matter were overruled."

She spoke quite calmly, not at all with the passion with which she had spoken about theatre, but there was a well of emotion beneath her words. The phrase *marital relations* was not one that she would use lightly.

"It's not that," I said. "It was more about the museum collection."

"Oh." Miss Horniman was thrown, having been so sure that she knew what I had come about. I had surprised her a second time. While she was wrong footed, I made my move.

"I wanted to ask about your upbringing—being brought up with those things all around you," I said. "An Aladdin's cave of the esoteric. What was it in there that woke you to the larger world?"

"What a question..." But her expression softened, and she brushed back a hair. "Father did not allow us to have friends, so my brother Emslie and I played among the mummy cases and the African masks. We made up our own friends. The Chaldean idols, and Hyperborean bas-reliefs, and South Seas jujus were our playmates, and we made adventures among them. Osiris and Ganesha were members of the household."

"But was there something specific that kindled your interest in... the other world?"

"To me it was always as normal as a greengrocer's," she said, ignoring me. "More ordinary, in fact, because we were surrounded by emissaries from the other world, and we never had to go out shopping. I never saw the inside of a greengrocer's until I went to art school. That must seem very strange to you."

It must have been a strange, lonely existence. Her father, I recollected, had been a strict adherent to some obscure religious sect. That was why she was not allowed to play with other children and was educated privately at home with her brother.

"It seems like a long time ago. Theatre is a better sort of magic, in the end. McGregor went mad, they say—too much contact with those chthonic beings on the astral plane scrambled his brains."

I gathered that the name McGregor meant Liddell Mathers. She did not sound especially sorry for him.

"But I can see you're determined to do your research, Mr Stubbs, and determination is no bad thing for a writer. It doesn't drive everyone mad. Arthur used to spin his yarns off what he learned in the Golden Dawn, and it didn't harm him."

Arthur could only mean Arthur Machen, one of her fellow initiates in the Golden Dawn. He was a noted writer of fantastic stories, which were not perhaps as fantastic as I had thought when I first read them. Machen had laughed at the eccentricities of the Golden Dawn, but he understood their grasp upon the human psyche. He thought that what they saw were just shadows. Others, like Yeats and Mathers and Miss Horniman, believed that there was something casting those shadows.

"Well, I'm getting used to being represented in fiction," Miss Horniman went on. "Just make sure you get me down properly, 'warts and all' as the Protector had it."

"I'll do my utmost."

"Spoken like a man," she said drily. I had a feeling it was not the first time she had delivered that particular backhanded compliment. "Well, I'm afraid it's not much of a story… but I shall try to oblige you. I must have been ten years old at the time, so Emslie would have been seven. We were playing a game in among all the lumber—this was before the first museum was built and everything was stored higgledy-piggledy around the house. We loved it that way, but it drove my poor mother to distraction—not that she would ever say anything when yet another cartload of strange boxes arrived from Nepal or Valparaiso, but you could tell she was wondering where we would put it.

"Emslie wanted to be a Roman soldier, and he needed a helmet. Nothing was right; we had all sorts of hats but not one that would satisfy him. Then he saw this African idol from the Congo—it's a frightful sort of thing, made of brass decorated with hair, like a sort of egg-shaped human figure—and he wanted it."

In the way she recounted the anecdote, Miss Horniman sounded like frustrated storyteller. Her role in theatre had always been as a patron, a theatre manager, and an organiser. She'd had little chance to participate in the creative process, and her own stories had remained pent up inside her. A person working with W. B. Yeats and George Bernard Shaw did not get much of a chance to hold forth.

She continued to describe the argument between her and Emslie. "I told him, 'Don't be ridiculous. You can't wear that.'

"And Emslie absolutely bawled at me, 'I want his helmet!'

"'It's all one piece,' I said.

"'No, it isn't!' He was quite purple by that time. 'The top comes off!' he said.

"And when I looked more closely, he was quite right. There was a hairline crack between the top half of the idol's head and the rest. I tried to get it off, but it wouldn't budge, so I found some scissors, and I wedged the point in and tried to prise it open with Emslie urging me on.

"At first, it wouldn't come at all, and I broke one point off the scissors, and I knew I would be punished for that. And then I thought, well, I've nothing to lose now, so I tried with the other point.

"Somehow, I managed to lever it open just a little tiny way… the room was dark, and I so vividly remember the line of light peeking through from the inside of the idol as though it was full of fire. It wasn't a light or a sound, but it was something like the buzzing of bees.

"I was terrified, and I pushed down on the top and shut off the light and ran away. Emslie burst into tears and ran after me, and we hid among the antelope furniture. We stayed hidden for ages until I felt safe again.

"I never spoke to Emslie about it afterwards, and I don't

know what he saw or heard or whether he even remembered the occasion. A few days later, I asked my father what the idol was. He was always very fond of explaining things in his collection, and he found the letter that had come with it. It had been recovered by a missionary in West Africa... there was a colony of lepers on an island in a river that worshipped it. They said it contained a stone that had fallen from the sky. What the Greeks called a baetyl."

"I've heard the term," I said.

"The lepers were white, and the natives assumed the missionary was one of them, so they put him on this island with them. I can't remember the rest of the story, but the missionary escaped, and when he returned, he found that a band of Belgian slavers had come and killed all the lepers and burned down all their huts."

"Belgian slavers—why would they kill lepers?"

"I don't know, and I don't know how they knew the men were slavers, but that's what everyone said," she said, frowning at the point. "They were masked, I remember that, and led by Europeans, anyway. But the slavers didn't find where the idol was hidden. The missionary brought it back."

"Why would a Christian missionary bring back something like that?"

"Even Christians can't always ignore the truth when they stumble on it. I think he was torn between wanting to destroy it and wanting to build a shrine to it as the relic of an unknown saint. He couldn't do either, so he gave it to Father, who was a notorious collector of old gods."

"And did you tell Mathers and the others about it?"

She hesitated a moment. "I didn't," she said at last. "Truth to tell, I forgot about it for a long time. After that, I assumed the whole incident had been childish fancy and imagination. It was only after I ascended in the Golden Dawn that I began to understand what it was—and by that time, I had broken with Father and Emslie. I would have cut off my right arm before I'd ask them for anything. No, I've never told anyone about it. Except perhaps the odd friend or two over the years."

Mabel Brown was an ambitious woman who had wanted to

get on in the theatre and had gone to seek her fame in the West End. Perhaps she had become a protégé of Annie Horniman, and perhaps, in the course of worming her way into Miss Horniman's inner circle, she had learned something that would later be to her advantage when she came across Stafford's advertisement.

"It's a wonderful story," I said.

"Theatrically speaking, it's only half a story, or one act at best. It needs an ending. I'm sure Arthur would write a good ending to it."

"I'll see what I can manage," I said.

Chapter Fifteen

The Coal-Hole

I had never been party to planning a major robbery before. Thanks to Miss Horniman, we knew the exact room and the case where the baetyl lay. The only difficulty was getting our hands on it. My first impulse—to advise Stafford to make a bid for it—quickly ran into the sand and not just because Stafford was unwilling to do anything openly.

Even if we could have found a surrogate gentleman buyer, there was a more substantial obstacle: it was not in the power of the museum director to simply sell items. Any such actions would need to be ratified by the board of trustees, who only met infrequently and who were in the business of building up and maintaining a collection, not selling things off. Money was not a motive for them, and as Skinner pointed out, even if we offered them a thousand pounds, that would simply reinforce the impression that the idol was worth holding on to.

"They'd want to take a closer look at it," said Skinner. "And what happens when they open it up to look inside? 'Bring in the bottled lightning, a clean tumbler, and a corkscrew'—light the blue touch paper and stand well back when they unbottle that!"

If they did open the idol, the quantity of lightning it drew would surely be far greater than the small piece that Mabel Brown extracted. I was forced to agree that, like Mabel Brown, we would have to obtain the item by illicit means.

Breaking into a museum was a rather different proposition to breaking into a house. As I had often noted, with houses, the protection was often of a symbolic nature, and the security measures were informal. A museum was by definition a repository of valuable items, and the protection was correspondingly formidable.

A house might have locks on the doors and windows, but those fitments themselves were not usually so solid that they couldn't be opened with a pry bar wielded by a hand skilled in that art. It was more a question of how quickly and quietly the thing might be achieved. And a museum, even a small one like the Horniman, would have iron bars on the windows and doors that would not yield to manual implements. Moreover, it would inevitably employ a night watchman, and these days, museums were likely to have electric alarms which responded when doors or windows were opened, so that even the most inattentive guardian would be aroused from his doze and alerted to the presence of intruders.

Furthermore, the display cases themselves, especially those housing the more valuable exhibits, might have their own alarms. Some of those were silent so you did not know when you had tripped one. Now that the telephone was universal, a watchman could summon the law instantly without getting up from his comfortable chair. The metropolitan police could dispatch a flying squad in a fast car, and the end result would be a firm hand on your shoulder while you are still engaged in the act of burglary.

While I had effected entries to many places in the course of recovering debts, a museum was in a different league than anything I had previously essayed. I found the prospect daunting.

By contrast, Skinner, who had much less experience in that field than I, was not troubled in the least. "It's a piece of cake, Harry. This isn't the Bank of England; it's a ruddy museum."

"It's an act of outright robbery," I said. "It's not like we can say that we are recovering the idol on behalf of someone with a better claim to it, and breaking and entering means seven years hard labour. And if you've got your knife on you—a *deadly weapon,* in legal parlance—the tariff will be increased by five years."

"'Tariff,'" he said scornfully. "You talk far too much like a policeman, Harry, and not enough like a proper criminal. And pry bars aren't the way to do it! I suppose I'll have to educate you in the ways of theft."

Later that day, I returned from an errand to find Skinner working with a school printing set. It was one of those kits provided with an ink pad and letters, cut out of rubber, that fit into a frame. He was moving with utmost care.

"You won't get very far by pretending to be something you're not," Skinner said with the air of an oracle. "The trick is to pretend to be something you are."

As an apprentice in the arts of deception, I accepted that without comment.

"If you or I—and might I say, particularly you—was to attempt to pass yourself off as a scholarly, upper-class gent, you'd have less chance than a chicken in a coop full of foxes. Those types speak their own language, and they can spot an impostor as easily as we'd spot a lord pretending to be a workman down at the Conquering Hero. But if you pretend to be what you are…"

He stamped the letters firmly down and lifted them up after a second.

"What am I?" I asked.

"You're a man who goes around retrieving valuable items for other people, of course. And if I was to be casting for a stage performance, I couldn't ask for a man who more looks the part."

Skinner inspected his newly created letterhead with a magnifying glass. He had already spoiled several sheets of vellum, flicking them irritably onto the floor when he discovered imperfections.

"That's more like it." He put the sheet carefully to one side. "The other thing is not to let them know what you really want. That was where we went wrong with Higgs. Conceal your true intentions so they go protecting the wrong things and thinking they've thwarted you while you waltz off with what you're actually after."

He stamped the second sheet with equal care.

"Have you done this sort of thing before?" I asked.

"The same general principles apply, whatever the specifics."

Skinner's plan involved sending a series of letters to the

museum from a fictitious government department. They all used a similar letterhead, so creating a simulacrum of an official document was not too difficult. With typical nerve, he had even borrowed one of my ideas: he suggested that the idol might be dangerously radioactive. He would imply that radioactivity had been discovered in a similar idol in a museum in the Gambia—which, of course, would be impossible to check—and that it would be necessary to remove said item for a thorough scientific inspection.

Skinner used a genuine address belonging to the Ministry of Agriculture so that any letters of response would be shuttled around Whitehall's endless corridors for weeks before being returned to the sender. By which time we would have achieved our objective.

"All you and I have to do is impersonate a couple of glorified furniture-removal men with government pensions," said Skinner. "A copy of the letter as our authorisation, and Bob's your uncle."

"But what if they challenge us?"

He smiled indulgently. "People like that don't argue with government officials! Not with us threatening them with putting a safety cordon around the whole museum. No, we'll give them a nice receipt with an official stamp and a reference number on it—I've printed a couple of forms—and they'll think they got off lightly."

I must have looked sceptical, but Skinner was ready with an ace up his sleeve.

"Because we have this." He opened his hand to reveal a small brass tube, which he aimed at me like a telescope. He inspected the other end and pretended to adjust it. "Oh, yes. Oh, yes. I'm seeing dangerously high levels of Z-rays coming out of your body, Mr Stubbs. It's reading forty-five, and that's terribly high."

"What is that device?"

"It's a scientific radiometer," he said, pleased as a schoolboy with a new magnifying glass. "I borrowed it off the boss. You can't argue with science."

"I can't, but the museum people might know how to read it."

"I hope they do," he said. "I've got one of the test samples that comes with it stuffed inside, so it reads high."

"Doesn't he mind you breaking his radiometer?" As soon as I asked, I knew Stafford would have handed over a hundred radiometers to be crushed if he could get one step closer to the baetyl. Miss De Vere was right about him in at least one way: he would scruple at nothing—whether it was throwing his fortune away, employing a rogue like Skinner, or seeing his staff wasting away—if it would bring his Holy Grail to him.

"If it doesn't work," I said, "and if they get suspicious, we'll be nabbed on the spot."

"Not likely. You'll knock the block off anyone who gets in our way. And we can do a smash-and-grab, get the idol, and be away before they know what's hit them." Skinner laughed merrily, giving me the impression he might actually prefer a ruckus and us running out, clutching our prize, chased by outraged men in black uniforms. He liked to create a bit of chaos. But he would be pleased enough just to outsmart them with his ruse and his radiometer.

"Now," said Skinner, looking again at the letterhead he had created. "What we need are some words to put on this. Why don't you go to the library and see if you can get one of those books of professional form letters for us? You know the sort of thing. We've got to get it just right so as not to arouse suspicion."

And so, with a little help from Skinner, over the next few days I drafted and wrote the letters in my best copperplate hand, perfected during my brief career as a legal clerk. One letter would not be enough; Skinner believed that verisimilitude required at least three, coming from more than one department. His approach was slapdash. I made careful note of the names of the supposed officials and their roles and used a different pen with subtly altered handwriting when writing from a different office.

It was a long and painstaking business, but there was little else to occupy us apart from a reduced round of routine duties. Stafford had lost interest in the other activities. The only interruption came when a taxi arrived late one afternoon with another urgent summons.

"Our social standing is rising by the day," said Skinner. "He's inviting us into the house now."

On our third visit to the Firs, we were admitted into the main building by the butler and shown into a downstairs drawing room. I had little time to take in the details; the floor was a plain, polished parquet, and the lights were classical female figures holding globes aloft. Stafford stood in front of the marble fireplace, which had a spray of peacock feathers in place of a fire. He looked ill at ease.

"Good of you to come," he said. "Another problem with Pierce, I'm afraid. We thought he was calming down, but..."

"Has he got out again?" asked Skinner.

"There has been a lot of noise from the cellar," said Stafford. "I didn't think it was advisable to go down on my own."

"Very close quarters," said Skinner, nodding wisely. "You did the right thing. Difficult to swing a shotgun around in a confined space, and if he grabs the barrel, the game's up. You'd best leave this to us, sir."

The prisoner was confined in a locked room in the cellar. There had been some loud sounds an hour previously, followed by silence. None of the staff dared to go down and check on him; the gardener who had previously assisted us said that indoors was none of his job.

Stafford waited at the top of the stairs, shotgun in hand, as we descended.

"I fear for young Pierce's health," said Skinner in an undertone as we descended the stairs. "He wasn't a well man the last we saw of him. If we find a body, you can bet that muggins here is going to be asked to get rid of it."

I had some previous experience in that line myself, but I held my tongue.

At the bottom of the stairs was a short corridor with a bare electric light bulb. Four doors led off it. The one on the left, normally a store for root vegetables from the garden, was Pierce's prison cell.

"Evening, Pierce," Skinner said. "Stubbs and I have come to see how you are. Your people are worried about you."

There was no reply. No sound at all except our breathing.

Skinner slipped the key into the lock, and I readied myself. He had advised me that I must not let myself be bitten or spat upon; we would need to subdue Pierce quickly.

Skinner turned the handle, and I nudged the door open with my toe. Inside, it was dark. The light from the corridor outlined ambiguous shapes.

"Hello, Pierce," I called.

"Let's shed some light on the matter." Skinner coolly reached around into the dark room, feeling for the light switch. It would have been the perfect opportunity for an ambush if Pierce had been lying in wait. Skinner was betting against that.

The light clicked on to reveal a low-ceilinged cellar room that was bare, apart from a pallet in one corner with a jug and similar items near to it. From our viewpoint outside the room, there was no sign of the prisoner.

"He's gone," I said.

"He can't have done," said Skinner. "He must be up against the wall, where we can't see him, or behind the door."

I nodded then jumped into the room and pivoted round in a crouch, ready to confront Pierce. He was not there.

The room smelled terrible—not just the lavatorial smell of a place where a man has been locked up with only the most primitive means of hygiene, but an acrid, chemical smell that stung my nose. Heating pipes ran along the far wall and up through the ceiling. A heavy chain, which had presumably restrained the prisoner, still hung from them, trailing on the mattress.

It did not take long to discover his means of escape. Airbricks between this cellar and the adjacent one had been removed and the mortar around them scraped away. The gap this labour had created did not look large enough for a man to crawl through, even a youth like Pierce, but there was no other explanation.

Skinner and I looked through to the dark beyond.

"It goes into the coal-hole," I said as I made out the glitter of light off the facets of the coal piled high.

If the coal cellar had been full, removing the air bricks would have brought the pieces tumbling through into Pierce's cell, but this being the height of summer, there were only a couple of feet of coal in the bottom of the hole.

"It must be fed from a chute above, at the back of the house," I said. "Either he's still in there, or he got out through the coal chute."

Before we left, I went to look at the chains. I wished to glean something of how Pierce had freed himself. The answer was simpler and more grisly than I would have guessed. The heavy chain, which might usually have been used to secure gates or other openings, had been fastened around Pierce's leg. He had not picked the lock, sawed through it with a file, or prised it apart; it was still secure. Pierce's foot was still there in the chains, ripped off cleanly at the ankle. Like an animal that gnawed through its own leg to escape a trap, Pierce had torn himself loose.

As with the thumb in the flowerbed, there was no blood, and the edge of the torn flesh was dry and powdery rather than bloody. The foot might have been a lump of clay rather than a once-living thing.

"Christ almighty," said Skinner, turning away from it.

The hatch from the corridor to the coal cellar was too small to admit a person, so we went upstairs, offering a few words of explanation to Stafford.

Above the coal-hole was a chute that led up to a manhole cover. To open the cover from above, we needed a lifter key—a T-shaped steel instrument with an end that fit into a recess in the manhole cover. After a brief search in the household, we duly discovered that tool.

The other staff stood back while I opened the cover and Skinner shone a torch into the cellar below. He flicked the light this way and that. The bare floor showed under a scant covering of coal; perhaps a man might have concealed himself under it, but there was a more obvious alternative.

"What do you reckon, Harry?" Skinner asked in an undertone.

A man standing in the coal-hole could take hold of the ends of the chute, and if he was wiry enough, he could wriggle up the narrow chute, bracing himself against the metal sides with arms and legs. At the top, opening the manhole cover would be simply a matter of pushing upwards with sufficient force. The lifter key was only needed to gain purchase from above; there was no bolt. A small, determined man might have done it, especially one who had already forced his way through that small hole in the wall.

I knelt down to inspect the sides of the manhole. There was a scraping of whitish, powdery material on one edge. Surely, they would have heard the cover move; but that was probably one of the loud noises that had alarmed Stafford.

"Gone," said Skinner, eyeing the white residue.

"Are you telling me he got clean away?" asked Stafford, unable to believe it.

"He did get clean away, sir," said Skinner.

Stafford turned from us but not before we saw the agitation in his features. He was far out of his depth in a situation he did not fully understand, and he had nobody to turn to—except us.

"Would you like us to track him down?" Skinner asked.

"By all means—if you can," said Stafford, gazing out into the darkness over the lawns. I stood up. The summer air was fresh and sweet after the chemical reek from the cellars. "I don't understand it. He doesn't have anywhere else to go… we must get that idol as soon as possible."

"We were planning on collecting it next week," said Skinner.

"Make it tomorrow morning," said Stafford, looking into the sky as though the stars were an hourglass that showed time running out. "I don't care what it costs. It must be before tomorrow night."

"First thing tomorrow morning," Skinner affirmed.

"The Grail," he said. "Time is short. If only I could explain to you what it means!"

I felt we already had some understanding of what it meant, based on its effects on Pierce and Miss De Vere's warnings. Stafford must have read the doubt in our faces.

"The physical effect is not important. It is the spiritual effect, a transformation, a transubstantiation…" He raised his hands and lowered them again. "A link between man and heaven."

We left him looking up into the sky and wondering at the stars.

To Skinner, the turn of events was not unwelcome if it meant a little extra money. And I did not doubt that finding Pierce would be another task above and beyond the call of duty for which an additional gratuity would be forthcoming.

The butler escorted us down the gravel path, and my eyes sought out the greenhouse, which had been bursting with unnatural growth. It was empty. The lush vegetation had vanished, turned to powder, just as Pierce probably would be in a few days.

"The kindest thing would have been to put him out of his misery," Skinner said with a brutal simplicity. "I know men who survived gas attacks and died slow. Ah, there you go, looking all offended now, but you know it's the truth."

The butler solemnly unlocked the great front gate for us. Skinner inspected the bars as he did so. They were too close-set for any except the smallest and skinniest burglar to squeeze through, but the gap was not so narrow as the opening in the coal-hole wall.

"Don't bother locking the stable door, pal," Skinner told the butler. "The horse has bolted. But we'll get him back for you."

Chapter Sixteen

Streatham Fair

I had suggested renting a van for our expedition. It would be easy enough to get an anonymous black vehicle, one that might have belonged to any government function. I felt it would make our entrance more convincing, but Skinner said it was unnecessary, as nobody would be following us in and out of the museum. He did, however, agree to a taxi to throw off any of Elsie Granger's mob who might be dogging our footsteps.

As we crossed the car park, Skinner jerked a thumb at a glazier's van. "That might have been an easier way of gaining admission. Plumbers, builders, glaziers, gasmen. All you need are some overalls, and you can get in anywhere."

I wondered why the glazier would be visiting when my eye fell on another vehicle.

"More importantly," I said, "we have been anticipated."

Skinner followed my gaze to the limousine parked across the way. The passenger window was rolled down. When we hesitated, a red-nailed hand beckoned us over.

"Morning, ma'am," said Skinner, touching his hat. "You received my message?"

"The idol's gone," Miss De Vere said. "The museum was broken into last night. The case with the idol was broken, among others. They haven't noticed the idol is missing yet."

"Did the night watchman see—"

"Oh, he saw something all right," she said. "When we could eventually get him to talk—and it wasn't easy—he said he'd seen a mummy."

"A mummy?" Skinner asked.

"Pale, ghastly, withered. Usual get-up."

"How did you get involved?" It was not my place to ask, being only the assistant of an assistant, but I was carried away by events.

"I'm a psychologist," she said patiently, "specialising in trauma cases. Naturally, the police recommended me as I happened to be in the area."

"This mummy," said Skinner. "He didn't happen to have a foot missing?"

"It was hobbling along with some difficulty," she said. "But it hit the night watchman hard enough to crack his ribs. He was in a state of shock, and I had to sedate him." She gave an ironic smile. "They're checking that all the mummies are still there, just to make sure."

"Do you know what it means?" Skinner asked.

"Yeah," she said in a tired voice. "The flock are coming home to roost. You'd better get in."

The limousine had the same arrangement of seating as a taxi, so we were able to sit facing Miss De Vere on folding chairs, presumably intended for attendants or bodyguards. Even with my bulk, the interior was roomy.

The driver faced rigidly away from us, eyes front, seemingly deaf.

We waited for Miss De Vere to speak.

"We have two sites of infection," she said. "The meteorite inside the idol, and a contaminated source of water. Probably a pool, a well, or a spring that your gipsy woman knew about. If Pierce takes the idol to the water, they will combine. We need to stop that."

She stopped, apparently bored at having to recite this to us.

"Because they'll turn this place into the Sahara Desert?" Skinner prompted.

"Perhaps."

"And the gipsy, Madam Hester," I said. "There was a fire…"

"One less problem to worry about," she said.

"We need to stop Pierce from getting to the water," said Skinner. "How do we find him? Dogs…?"

"You won't find him," she said. "What you need to do is locate the source of the water and wait for him. He can't move around in daylight."

I forbore to point out that Madam Hester had been our best lead to finding the water.

"If I may ask another question," I said. Miss De Vere turned her gaze on me as though I was an irksomely persistent child. "When one of these meteorites comes down to earth, unless it's inside a metal container, it attracts lightning. The material disintegrates and gets into the water and may be absorbed by living things, changing them. Is that correct?"

She moistened her lips and paused before answering. "It does *change* things. If you want to expand your word power, the correct term is *teratogenic*. It eats through and replaces adult tissue, and it mutates growing tissue. It… makes monsters."

"What I do not understand," I said, "is how and why the two pieces would come together. Is there an intelligence guiding it? "

She sighed then spoke in quick, clipped tones.

"You might say it has a mind, or it is a mind. Not human. More like an ants' nest. A million fragments, discontinuous but cohesive."

A million fragments. Pierce had talked of Legion in his brain, Legion being the group of demons that Jesus cast out of the Gadarene swine. Before I could frame my next question, Miss De Vere spoke again.

"But that's not the point. Your Mr Darwin was pretty clear about survival… kill or be killed. When a seed lands on a desert island, it either grows into a plant and makes more seeds, or it dies. We stamp seeds out."

"If it's intelligent, we could communicate with it… perhaps."

A muscle in her jaw flexed, then relaxed. "It's not like us," she said calmly. "It doesn't know we even exist. It will destroy us without thinking. But actions speak louder than words. Extermination is easy to understand, even for something that doesn't think the way we do."

"This town ain't big enough for the both of us," said Skinner in a bad American accent.

Miss De Vere did not smile.

"If the Indians had killed every white man who landed, they'd still own America," she said. "You know the word *ambiguous*? How about *unambiguous*? I'd like to send it an unambiguous message."

"I see," I said.

"You'll need to neutralise what's gotten into the gardener," she said, taking something from her bag and passing it to me. It looked like a boiled sweet wrapped in cellophane, making me feel more than ever like a child with a teacher.

"Does he have to eat it?" I asked.

"Just throw it at him."

I held it up. It might have been a translucent yellow-brown barley sugar round as a marble. I tried to pass it to Skinner, as leader of the party, but he refused.

"If only we had some way of finding the water." I recalled Madam Hester's tea reading and Yang's divination. "Can you do anything?"

"I am doing something." She looked at Skinner. "You know how to find it."

It was the first I had heard of it. But perhaps Miss De Vere was more expert at reading people's unspoken thoughts.

"Assuming your offer of a bounty if we can get the idol still holds good," he said, smoothing his moustache, "I think I have an idea."

"How?" I asked.

Skinner smiled enigmatically.

Miss De Vere nodded, more to herself than to us, and pushed the latch to open the car door. "I'll see you boys tomorrow when you have it."

Outside in the car park, Skinner seemed unusually animated. "Harry my boy," he said, slapping me on the shoulder, "you and I are going to the fair."

"Should we tell Stafford?"

The argument over whether we would be dealing with Stafford or Miss De Vere had never been resumed, but Skinner seemed untroubled.

"I'll drop him a line to let him know we're on the trail," he said. "Now then, this is where it gets interesting."

The bus to Streatham Common was crowded with people in a holiday mood. The schools were out, and it seemed that everyone had children with them. Wary, I squeezed myself into a corner to keep from accidentally crushing any stray toddlers underfoot. At the junction with the High Road, we all spilled out like a seedpod bursting, and Skinner and I allowed ourselves to be carried along with the crowd through the archway and into the summer fair.

The fairground was a cheerful chaos of steam calliope music and swirling crowds fired up with excitement by gaudy colours and the barkers outside every tent and every ride. A giant papier-mâché clown with a red nose welcomed everyone in. Vendors hawked candyfloss and toffee apples and paper cones of monkey nuts. Parents waved to their children as they spun past on the merry-go-round, and there were shrieks from the camel ride as two girls were hoisted into the air.

Three boys ran past, shouting and laughing, contributing to the air of near riot. It was a scene of carnival, bringing back memories of those happy days before the war when there was nothing better than to be a boy in a fairground with a shilling your pocket. How my brother and I always looked forward to the day the fair arrived. The posters would go up two weeks before, and then another lot of posters one week before, and we would count the days.

"The old gaff! Like coming home, isn't it?" said Skinner, beaming at the whole performance. "Just keep your eyes open now, because I would be surprised if we were not being followed."

We sauntered through the row of shooting galleries and watched men trying to impress their sweethearts by shooting painted ducks with an air rifle.

"Tuck that elbow in, soldier!" Skinner instructed cheerfully in his sergeant's voice after one fellow missed three in a row. "And don't hold your breath when you aim."

The man shot him a dirty look, but Skinner just laughed, and a second later, the would-be marksman laughed back just as loud. Even shooting was a frivolous business at the fair, and rifles meant larking about for teddy bears, not trench warfare.

I jerked my head, indicating I had spotted a man watching us from two stands over. Skinner nodded and moved on.

"Where are we going?" I asked.

"I'm going to take you on the Grand Tour. See whether our shadow can stand the pace. Now then, where's that Hanson put his slanger this year?"

He headed off purposefully past a row of spinning tombola wheels, each offering more lavish prizes than the last. Seeing someone he recognised manning one of the stalls, he exchanged some words, few of which I understood. Then he set off briskly and turned at a sign pointing to Freddie Hanson's Sporting Academy. It read, "England's Premier Pavilion—All Comers Challenged."

"You just follow my lead, Harry," Skinner said, lifting the flap. "I'll show you how to make a bit of pocket money."

The man following us—the ferret-faced man from the museum, I now saw—hesitated to come in, put off no doubt by the entrance fee.

There must have been forty or fifty men in the tent, filling half the benches. The boxing ring was a crude affair, just four posts driven into the ground joined by some stout rope with sawdust over the muddy ground.

A big, bearded man who could have been Russian or Turkish sat scowling on a stool in one corner. His cape was not drawn fully about him, and he had as much hair on his body as a bear. It did not disguise how flabby he was. Fairground boxers did not need to be athletes, but he looked right out of condition. Two other boxers, neither of them close to their prime, were having a low-voiced conversation with the seated man.

In the other corner was a knot of excited young men, one of them with his shirt off and his friends lacing up the boxing gloves for him. He looked far more athletic than his opponent, with a good set of muscles on him and a decent reach. He might have been boxing champion at his school or in his platoon, but he would need more than that to escape a beating. Carnival fighters were old pros and full of tricks to catch out an amateur. They also weighted their gloves while the challenger might find his gloves lighter than regulation. And they could get in plenty of low blows without the referee paying any heed—a referee whose count was faster or slower depending who he was counting for.

The barker, easily recognised by his scarlet waistcoat, was conferring at a side table with the ticket seller.

"You're just in time, gentlemen—sixpence each. Take any seat you like."

"As a matter of fact, we were seeking participation rather than observation," said Skinner.

The barker's smile fell when he saw me. "No, no," he said, raising a hand. "No professionals. It's strictly against the rules."

"Rules?" asked Skinner mildly. "A guinea for the man who can last three minutes in the ring—that's what it says on the board outside. There ain't no small print on it."

The barker looked again at Skinner. "Here, don't I know you?"

"Our paths may have crossed," said Skinner. "And I don't recall owing you any favours. Harry, go see if they've got gloves big enough for you."

The boxers were looking round at that point. I was being sized up. I stood to attention and looked coolly back at them then cracked a knuckle.

"No professionals," insisted the barker.

"My friend may be a past master in the noble art, but that's nothing to you," said Skinner, arms folded. "And you know how much the flatties like to see a real fight. They'll be very disappointed if I tell them you won't allow it."

Skinner had a shrewd understanding that the crowd would take his side and that the barker would be barracked at best. At worst, the crowd might start demanding their money back or damaging the place.

The barker scowled. "What do you want?"

Skinner looked at the ticket seller's wooden box with its slots for coins of different denominations. "My friend is very partial to a pint or three, and we couldn't help noticing the beer tent back there. Maybe a drink would soothe the disappointment of not getting a match."

The barker practically growled at this extortion, but he was first and foremost a pragmatic man. He wordlessly held up two shillings.

"Your very good health, Mr Hanson, sir," said Skinner brightly, touching his forefinger to his hat brim. "Harry, follow me to the pavilion of foaming tankards!"

We left quickly through the side entrance reserved for the boxers. Nobody stopped us. We were walking fast, turning and turning again and weaving through the crowd. A roar from behind us announced that the bout had started. We had left our pursuer outside the main entrance to the boxing tent, probably not wanting to part with sixpence. He had not seen our premature exit. And if he should ask, they would probably direct him to the beer tent.

Once we were well clear, Skinner stopped and broke into laughter, which was lost in the swirl of carnival noise. "Did you see old Freddie's face? Did you? What a glorious piece of business that was," he said, chuckling. "I owed him that."

"For a minute, I thought you were serious about me getting in the ring."

"What, let Freddie see his man take a beating, and lose a guinea into the bargain? Not likely. We could have got twice as much from the old skinflint." He pressed the coins into my hand. "Here you go, Harry. Money well earned. Buy yourself a toffee apple for starters."

"A grown man can't walk around eating a toffee apple."

"Get two of them, and I'll show you how it's done. Go on. He's selling them over there. That's an order, Bombardier Stubbs!"

We walked on down a row of sideshows, each of us chewing a sticky, crispy delicacy. I had not had a toffee apple for longer than I could remember; at some point, it had started to seem childish. Now the toffee apple felt like a small act of defiance against the world, and a very sweet and juicy act at that.

The main thing with a toffee apple is not to let it fall off the stick and be ruined. The sticks can be a bit haphazard. The makers of toffee apples do not take all the trouble they should, especially considering how many of their customers are small children who can be mortified by the loss of their sweet. The sight of us both earnestly nibbling made passers-by smile, and I smiled back.

Skinner paused to explain the economics of coconut shies. The secret was that coconuts could be bought wholesale for less than the penny that people paid for the chance to win one. Therefore, the game did not need to be as difficult as many of the other games though the use of hollow wooden balls meant that even a direct hit might not be sufficient to dislodge one.

"Now then," said Skinner. "That's where we're headed. Just let them finish leaving."

At first I thought he meant the *Torture* exhibition, which offered a display of instruments of torture and execution down through the ages with the aid of waxworks. Then, as we went past, I saw that the next tent down was our destination.

"Everett's Wonders of The Natural World" read the placard. "Nature's Most Astounding Freaks—You Will Be AMAZED."

Everett boasted a five-legged sheep, a two-headed snake—"both heads deadly poisonous"—a Fiji mermaid, and a variety of other stuffed and preserved specimens as well as the living *Horror of Horrors,* for which there was an additional charge.

I had seen carnival freak shows before. I expressed the view that while they might be sufficient to impress small children and the poorly educated, in these days of cinema newsreels they had to be struggling to keep up. Once all of us had seen a real duck-billed platypus, it wasn't enough to stitch together some random arrangement of animal parts.

"With this type of show, it's all in the patter," Skinner told me between bites of apple. "You don't just put the audience in front of a cage and let them look. You have curtains over the cage, and you build it up and get the anticipation going about how monstrous it is. And don't have too much lighting—keep it shadowy and suggestive. Let their imagination do the work, and feed it. And if you have a female accomplice to shriek and faint when it's uncovered, you'll get them all at it."

"You certainly know the carnival world."

"Ah, here we are." Skinner tossed his apple aside and darted forward as a man stepped from a side entrance of the freak-show tent. Everett, the show's proprietor, had a shaved head, wore a sort of black military uniform with a lot of silver braid, and carried a short swagger stick. The uniform was heavy; I sweated just to look at it. He bent down to splash water from a bucket over his face and head, and Skinner approached as he was wiping himself with a towel.

"Hullo, Bertie. You still joggering, then?"

"Well, if it isn't old Stinker," said Everett, not unfriendly but wary. He spoke with a Northern accent. "Who's this with you?"

"Harry's a pal—business partner." Skinner offered Everett our business card. "And for business reasons, we wanted to get a dekko at your star attraction."

Everett glanced at the card but did not take it. He clearly did not trust Skinner.

"Business reasons," said Everett. "Time's money. I don't give free looks, but you can come in if you pay, same as the rest."

I still had coins jingling in my pocket and passed over the requisite amount.

Everett took us inside. His displays were laid out inside the tent in a spiral. We passed the dim-lit alcoves—bright lighting was not a feature of freak shows—and came to the last one. That was behind a door, a peculiar fixture for a tent, secured with an outsize padlock and chain and plastered with lurid warning signs. Beyond was the *Horror of Horrors.*

For some reason, it made me think of Pierce in his cellar room.

"This is one-hundred-percent genuine," said Everett, tapping the door with his swagger stick. "This isn't a rigger; it's the real thing. What I usually do is I invite one of them to go first for free—some raklo who thinks he's seen it all and jeers at the other displays. When he comes out shuddering and gibbering, his friends just have to see what it is."

"And what is it?" I asked.

Everett undid the padlock. "Like no living thing you have ever seen before. You won't be happier for seeing it," he warned. "And remember what I tell all of my customers: what has once been seen cannot ever be unseen. You enter here at your peril."

"It's all in the warm-up," Skinner told me.

"Well, don't say I didn't warn you."

Behind the door was a small room, empty but for a table on which stood an object the size of a breadbasket covered by a black cloth. Everett poked his stick under the edge of the cloth, as though not wanting to get too close, and whisked the cover away with a dramatic swish.

"Behold the lagomorph," he said.

Underneath the cover was a wooden cage or hutch half-filled with straw. Something stirred inside, moving towards the wire mesh at the front.

I cannot describe what made it so repulsive, not in simple terms. It had four limbs in the right places, and it was symmetrical like any other animal. Nothing about it was especially monstrous, taken in isolation. A picture, even a photograph, would not have seemed particularly malformed. But in the way it moved, more in the way it looked at you, there was something that was not at all like any normal animal. The strangeness was in the way that every expectation was subverted.

The shock it gave was akin to looking into a crib and expecting to see a baby and instead finding a bloody aborted foetus—one that moved and lived and looked up with accusing eyes and worked its lips to speak to you.

A small nose and dark eyes gazed out at us through the wire mesh. I caught a glimpse of teeth, odd teeth like some mad carpenter's tools, and something made me look away suddenly before I saw its tongue.

Maybe all of it boiled down to this: the way it looked at us was so disquieting. Like no animal should ever look at you. The rest of it was perhaps incidental. I couldn't say, really, what it was, but the sight was so vile it seemed to imprint an after-image inside my eyeballs.

I heard Skinner catch his breath.

"You believe me now, don't you?" said Everett with grim pride. He replaced the cloth without looking at what was underneath. "This little monster is the reason I'm still in business. A real earner."

My sight felt as though it was stained. I wanted to look on clean things, on green fields and clouds and animals and people without deformity, and let the images wash my vision clean until everything was back to how it should be again.

It was incredible that such a thing would be on show, but the economic facts of life meant that people would take advantage of whatever they could. Madam Hester needed money, and any freakish animal was valuable to the proprietor of such a display. Skinner had correctly assumed that the cause of the water would lead to the effect showing up in Everett's tent.

"The only question is exactly where you got it from," said Skinner.

"My little secret," said Everett tapping his nose.

"We can pay."

Skinner contemplated a gold sovereign that had appeared in his palm.

Everett folded his arms, unmoved. He had told us that the monster was his livelihood, and the last thing he wanted was competition. The two men glared at each other for several seconds, neither wishing to be the first to break the silence.

"Madam Hester got it for you," I said.

Everett said nothing and did not look away from Skinner.

"I'm afraid my colleague here failed to explain our purpose, Mr Everett," I said. "We are not here for commercial motives. This is more of a humanitarian mission."

Everett gave a short, mirthless laugh. I could understand why he would not associate Skinner with such a cause.

Undaunted, I continued. "As you more than anyone can readily appreciate, this animal has undergone a horrible mutation from its natural form. It is not a normal sport of nature but a result of an alien influence, one that causes terrible modifications to living things. At present, it is confined to a single locality, but unless checked, it may become widespread."

"What?" His head jerked around.

"At present, it is only affecting woodland creatures. If it spreads, it will be not just animals and birds and cats and dogs but people as well. There will be babies born like that thing in there, or worse, if we don't stop it from going further."

"How do you know? You're not the proper authorities any more than I am. You're not telling me he"—Everett jabbed a disrespectful thumb towards Skinner— "is working for the police."

"Nevertheless," I said, "if it means anything to you, you have my solemn word that we will not share the information, and it will not be used for any mercenary ends."

He did not look convinced.

"This is a bad business," I said. "I've seen a man struck by lightning and a woman reduced to ashes. And Madam Hester, the fortune teller—"

"What do you know about her?"

"She died because of this. Personally, I'd advise you destroy that creature in there and never mention it to anyone again. If we found you, others can too."

Everett looked at me as though I was a dangerous madman.

"What is this?" he asked Skinner.

"More than I would have told you."

Everett ran a hand over his shaved head. "I knew it was uncanny. But… what's it to do with what happened to Madam Hester?"

"They want to keep the place secret," I said. "Anyone who knows is in danger. That includes you."

"And what's it to do with you?"

"We have undertaken to ensure that matters are concluded safely," I said. "No more deaths, and guilty parties brought to justice."

I caught Skinner's disbelieving look from the corner of my eye and ignored it. I had expected many more questions from Everett, but his mind did not work that way.

"Friggin'," Everett said. "She was burned down to nothing. It had to be murder, but the police didn't want to know. I knew the horror had to be too good to be true…" He shook his head. Long exposure to the monster had taken its toll, and a part of him, perhaps a large part, wanted to be well rid of it. Now we had supplied him with justification. "Here, do you have a pencil and paper?"

I handed Everett my notebook and a stub of pencil that I always keep ready. He sketched quickly and passed it back.

"That's Spa Hill there," he said. "X marks the spot. Madam

Hester took me there so I could put a trap down and catch that thing. She was getting half the take; that was the arrangement. I've not been back, but I know where it was."

"Is there water there?"

"Aye, a small pool. You won't mistake it, believe you me."

"Thank you," I said.

"You're a pal, Bertie," said Skinner.

"Just get out of my gaff, Stinker," said Everett. Then, to me, he said, "Your word of honour you're not tricking?"

"Word of honour," I said, holding out my hand.

We shook, and his grip was powerful.

"You think I need to change my line?"

"I would," said Skinner.

We left Everett looking troubled, tapping his knee with his swagger stick but already working on his next plan. It might not have been the first time he had a sudden change of career.

I was pleased to get out of the freak show, but the carnival mood had drained out of me. The music coming from different directions was discordant, and the smell of urine mingled with the candyfloss and toffee. The ground was littered with losing tombola tickets, and a man sat, weeping drunkenly, against a tent peg. The giant papier-mâché clown looked grotesque and ominous.

The image of that thing in the cage was still with me. My excitement had curdled into a dull sense of dread. Like a child who'd had too much running around and too many goes on the merry-go-round and too much candyfloss, I felt deflated, overstretched, and overtired.

"I thought we were going to have to tighten the screws on Bertie," said Skinner. "But you put the windup on him without so much as a raised fist."

"I didn't care for the look of that thing in the cage."

"Me neither," said Skinner, looking at his watch. "We've still got a few hours before H-hour. Time for a drink or two and some entertainment. There's dancing girls here, Harry."

Two women in oriental costumes were dancing listlessly outside a sideshow tent that promised "Dances of the World."

"They'll have a Turkish belly dancer, and a Polynesian

dancer with nothing but a grass skirt and a garland of flowers. That's always worth seeing, and"—he nudged me in the ribs—"the *Dance of the Seven Veils* at the end."

"I'm not in the mood," I said.

"Harry, do you want to die without ever seeing a naked woman?"

He laughed, but I turned away. We had found a way forward, thanks to his keen insight, but his flippancy was troubling.

"I was not planning on going to my death," I said.

"Nobody ever is. You can at least have a drink with me."

We headed for the crowded beer tent.That was the last time I ever had a pint with Skinner.

Chapter Seventeen

Night in the Woods

It was an exceptionally warm evening. Jackets and coats were out of the question, so we carried the essentials with us in leather satchels: electric torches, a storm lantern, some stout cord to bind Pierce with when we caught him, and flasks of water.

"Do you think it's dangerous?" I asked.

"Of course it's dangerous," said Skinner. "Otherwise, Miss Yankee Doodle Dandy would be front and centre. I called her on the phone, and she's leaving us to it."

"Perhaps she has other business."

"You can always tell something's up when the top brass decide they need to be somewhere else. Stafford knows something was up tonight, and something made Pierce tear his leg off to get out. I think we'll find him a changed man. Changed into what I wouldn't care to say."

I unwrapped the knuckledusters that I had retrieved from the bottom drawer in my lodgings. I was reluctant to employ them except in the most extreme circumstances, but it seemed we were coming to that.

There was a letter on my desk. One of the girls from the office next door must have left it. The address was written in Sally's handwriting, but the envelope was a plain one rather than her usual smart stationery.

"A billay-doo, eh?" said Skinner. "Always cheering to get one on the eve of battle."

"It's not a love letter."

There were several crossings-out and false starts, and it had obviously been written under considerable duress.

Dear Harry,

I am very sorry to be writing this.

I have to inform you that I am being held against my will.

My kidnappers say that to see me again you have to bring a certain object—they are sure you know what it is—to the Knyght's Head public house, and no funny business.

They say not to tell the police, and I am sure that you would not do that in any case.

I am safe and well and have not been harmed, but please, please do what they say.

Yrs as always,

Sally.

Elsie's thugs must have grabbed her on her way home from the factory, or maybe when she was out somewhere in the afternoon. They could not take on me and Skinner, but they could certainly handle a woman.

"That's low," said Skinner. "Though it is clever. You have to hand it to that Elsie."

"Kidnapped. This puts me in a difficult situation. If we get the idol, I'll need it to get Sally back."

Skinner smoothed his moustache but did not seem overly troubled. "Don't worry about it. It's all change after tonight anyway. Whatever happens, you and me are out of a job after this."

"I suppose so." I looked at the letter again as though rereading it would change the meaning.

"It's the truth. Except I'm not thinking of the labour exchange; I'm thinking of staying alive. Madame told us a lot today, things she never wanted to tell us before. She doesn't like it when people know too much. That can affect their life expectancy." He nodded solemnly.

"You really want to try and get the idol?" I asked.

"You're going to." He opened and closed his pocketknife, testing the smoothness of the action. "So I'd better come along and keep you out of trouble."

"What do we do?"

"We follow our instincts," Skinner said, "and we make it up as we go along."

The shadows were lengthening as we approached the woods, but it was still hot. The concrete pavement and the brick buildings were throwing back all the heat they had soaked up during the day. There was not a breath of wind, and it felt hotter than it had at noon. Every window was open, and families were sitting out on their doorsteps, quietly taking the evening air. Even the road had a tacky, melted look to it.

I patted my face with a damp handkerchief. Skinner turned Everett's map around in his hands, orienting it.

"So if that's Beulah Hill there, we want to go this way."

Under the trees, it was cool and shady. The heat of the day had not penetrated there. The path was hard mud, cracking in places from the lack of rain, and it led upwards through brambles and nettles under the great oaks. We walked slowly because of the temperature and the gradient.

"If you go down to the woods today," Skinner sang in a low voice, "you're sure of a big surprise..."

"We can't be far from the old Beulah Spa here. Same sort of phenomenon—a spring carrying particular minerals up from the depths. A spring that appears and disappears from time to time."

"Except you wouldn't drink from this one for your health," Skinner shot back.

Hoverflies struck sparks of light as sunbeams struck them in a clearing, and the spiderwebs glittered like silver mesh. Then we were in the green shade of the forest, stopping at intervals because the path was steep and we were still hot. Once a robin stopped on a branch a few feet away, cocked its head at me, and flitted away.

A lesser path, more of an animal track, led off to one side through the undergrowth. We stepped over a double strand of rusty barbed wire, all that was left of an old fence. Nobody had been that way in years.

Skinner found a stick and used it to beat his way along the track, beheading the nettles and thistles that crowded in on both sides.

I am sure that the possibility had occurred to him that Everett had sent us on a wild goose chase and even now was laughing at the thought of us stumbling around, bewildered, with thorns catching on our clothes.

We stopped for a swig of water, and I scanned the area methodically. I inspected the undergrowth, the tree trunks, and the leafy canopy for signs of malformation. The first things that caught my attention were the spiderwebs—not actual webs but individual long strands. I moved my head to make out more of them, and they radiated out at odd angles like the illustration in a geometry textbook. Ordinary spiders did not spin webs like that.

"It has to be near here," muttered Skinner.

"It is."

The fungus on a fallen log grew in long spikes; seen up close, they were faceted like diamonds and towered like a futuristic city in miniature, the little towers connected with horizontal bars unlike any fungus native to this planet. And they pulsed as though there was something moving within.

As I straightened up, something moved on a level with my face.

The earwig is a harmless creature, for all that people claimed it would crawl up their noses or in their ears when they were asleep. That was just a myth, and I had no objection to earwigs that minded their own business.

But this earwig was a big, brown, glistening thing as thick as my finger and as long as my forearm. It had far too many legs, and it snaked around a branch, feelers twitching in the air like whips. By the time I had realised what it was, the thing had slithered into a narrow crack in the tree. I did not have a chance to point it out to Skinner, but from the way he was scrutinising the ground by his feet, he must have found something similar.

"We're close," I said, still looking around, and pointed. "That way."

I do not know exactly what had attracted my attention about the one tree, but it was subtly altered. Like the monster that Everett displayed, there was nothing you could put your finger on, but the set of its branches and the arrangement of leaves were different to its neighbours.

"This one, you reckon?" Skinner gazed up warily.

A few feet from the tree, a spring broke the surface, and a thin trickle of water led to a pool that was more of a puddle. The vegetation around it was lush and unmistakably alien. Neither of us approached any closer.

I felt myself shiver. My sweat had cooled, leaving my shirt cold and clammy. I resisted the impulse to go back down the path and into the warmth.

Skinner was no more comfortable but made a show of cheerfulness. "So Bertie Everett is an honest man, and we'll be able to get this all wrapped up in time for last orders." Putting his satchel beside him, he brushed off a fallen log and sat down with an air of unconcern. "We've got a clear view of the path here, and we'll hear Pierce coming ahead of time."

I continued to stalk about quietly, cautiously examining the site. An earwig, even a monstrous one, was most likely harmless. Other creatures might be less benign.

The active agent only had the power to mutate things that were growing. The big oak, which must have been all of four feet in diameter, was two hundred years old or more and showed all the indications of having been infected. That spring had been bubbling up and then receding again for more than two centuries. Perhaps it had been there much longer, and one of Hester's predecessors had found it—maybe by noting the plants in the vicinity—and had discovered its unusual properties.

Paracelsus said that the gipsies knew many things unknown to scholars. What they used the water for, except making monsters for people like Everett, I could not imagine.

Forty years ago, a young boy had been rambling through these woods on a summer evening like this one, and he had seen blackberries unlike any other. He could not resist the temptation to try one. The taste must have been vile, but in the hours and days that followed, the active agent had worked its way into his system. He would never be able to find the spot again, and even if he had, the berries would have been gone, and the spring withdrawn again to subterranean regions.

The thing had been quiescent in his system for years, but

it had emerged again. Stafford had been seeking, like the poor man seduced by a faerie who vanished, the silver apples of the moon, the golden apples of the sun. Now he was able to grow them in his own greenhouse. Having seen the effects of ingesting a larger quantity, his desire to taste the fruit again might have abated, but perhaps not. To him, the changes it brought about might be a sacred transubstantiation—weak human flesh sloughed off as the Holy Spirit of alien fire burned through it.

"There go the last rays now," said Skinner as the canopy above us slipped into shadow. "You take your post the other side of the pool so we can catch him whichever way he comes in."

The light drained away almost imperceptibly, minute by minute. When we arrived, you could have read a newspaper by it, but without obvious change, the gloom had become so deep a person trying to read would have struggled with the headlines.

As the dark fell, the light that daylight had been masking gradually emerged. The glow was noticeable first directly over the pool, where it was brightest, but in fact, it suffused everything around us to a greater or lesser degree. The luminescence was so faint you could not be sure it was there until you looked twice. It had no colour at all, or rather, it was every colour mixed together. I can only describe it as being a grey light, impossible as that might sound.

"D'you see it? Like foxfire," I murmured. "Or will-o'-the-wisp."

"Like the corpse lights in Flanders," said Skinner.

The light over the pool shifted. I went to look into it. Shapes like ghostly goldfish congealed out of the surrounding water, swam a few strokes, and then, while going through a succession of shapes, slowly dissolved back into the pool. Watching it was hypnotic. There was a definite upwelling; the light was coming up from deep below. It cost me some effort to pull away and return to my post.

The trunk of the oak tree was limned in odd light, and it outlined the fern fronds. Little luminous blurs flowed over the vegetation. Perhaps a more poetic soul would have seen them as bespangled with angels' wings.

The light seemed to grow as the darkness settled in. That was probably an illusion, just as the moon that seemed pale in the blue sky in daytime was almost too bright to look at when the sky was midnight-black. We would not need our torches to see in the immediate vicinity of the big oak, although the lighting was as strange as a photographic negative, with the ground bright and the sky dark.

How much darker would it need to be before Pierce would come out? Surely he did not have far to go. Time always passed more slowly when you were waiting. If I had been able to read my watch, I doubt whether more than two minutes would have passed since I last wondered what the time was.

I made my own preparations, carefully unwrapping the cellophane that Miss De Vere had given me and holding the pellet in my hand. I noticed that it too had a faint glow, but dull red like an ember trapped in smoky glass.

"It's dark where you are," said Skinner.

Puzzled, I stood up, took a few steps, and looked back.

"The dark's following you," he said. "Like you was in a shadow."

I looked closely, and he was right. A bubble of darkness seemed to enclose me as though the light would not approach me closer than arm's length. At first, I thought it must be connected with the pellet, but a little experimentation showed the effect was centred on my person.

I could not account for it until I recalled the ring with its ancient gemstone on the chain around my neck. My collar was already unfastened, and I gingerly lifted the chain and placed the ring on the forest floor in front of me. Sure enough, the faint light dimmed where it rested. Whatever the alien forces were, they were clashing with each other. Perhaps that was inevitable, if Miss De Vere's view of Darwin and the struggle for supremacy was accurate. I conjectured that the makers of that stone were no friends of the meteorite riders, and the stone acted against their influence by some built-in mechanism.

I restored the chain around my neck.

A moth fluttered awkwardly past, blinking on and off, or

it might have been a dragonfly or a beetle. All I saw was the blur of its flight. The insect zigzagged past me a couple of times then circled Skinner several times, first clockwise and then anticlockwise.

"It's watching us," I said. "Everything here is part of its body. It suffuses every living thing here. It's waking up, putting out its feelers, and sniffing at us."

I heard a soft "thunk." Skinner had unclasped his knife and stuck it in the log next to him.

"I hope that isn't a sensitive part of its anatomy, then," he said, looking about.

"It's not in the dead wood, only the living vegetation and the insects."

"Hello," said Skinner, and we turned at a disturbance by the base of the oak.

The damp leaf mould, more organic humus than dirt, parted as something forced its way to the surface. I anticipated a nocturnal creature and braced myself for a monster to match the one in Everett's freak show, watching in spite of myself. Still, I could not see what it was. A formless head, perhaps rabbit sized but with no eyes or ears that I could make out, pushed loose and waved in the air. A second one broke the earth two feet away and rose up like a snake.

After a moment of confusion, I recognised it from the fingers. It was not a head but a hand on the end of an arm, and no sooner had I understood than the earth heaved, and the buried figure hauled itself out from a shallow grave of leaf mould.

It was hairless, all facial features eroded except for the deep cavities of eyeholes. I do not think it still had any clothes or any real surface or skin. Like a statue that had been worn down by centuries of wind and rain, its outline had softened. A normally decaying human soon withered away to the bones, but this had irregularities that did not indicate a human skeleton but some other form of internal scaffolding entirely.

Its presence underground made a kind of sense. Rather than allowing a usable human body to crumble away, as Pierce's was doing, the cadaver might be stored away against a time of need. And because the thing drew its energy from some alien source and had no need for food, or even air, a body could be buried for years or decades and brought to the surface at need.

As it clambered to its feet with unexpected agility, Skinner stuck his knife into the monster's chest and twisted.

That was not what I would have done.

I did not see exactly what happened next, but I had an overall impression of the earth erupting all around. Pale, flickering forms wrenched themselves out of the ground on every side, creatures that jerked like landed fish but with a weird synchronised quality, like a modern ballet troupe all carrying out their peculiar actions in time to unheard music.

Skinner was struggling with the first one to emerge. His knife was embedded deeply where its heart should have been, but it was grappling with him with too-flexible arms. It was stronger than him.

I'd stepped forward to try and separate the combatants when another of them grabbed Skinner from behind. It was huge, a giant of a man, and did not have proper hands—they had been lost—but the ends of its arms were split open into crude pincers.

Brambles caught at me, and even the tree branches seemed to entangle my arms as I fought free, as though I was in the clutches of a nightmare sea anemone in an underwater scene. Whether it was really grabbing me or that was just my fancy, my strength was great enough to tear myself loose from the vegetation.

Several of the creatures were moving to intercept me as I strode towards Skinner. They moved uncertainly, though, as if they could only sense me by smell. That must have been the effect of my bubble of darkness.

I could not win against coordinated opponents, but against a pack of blind men, I had a chance, and there were knuckledusters on my fists.

I kicked the first one solidly in the midsection as it approached. There was a surprising weight and density to it. The creature was not a dried-up husk like a mummy but had more the mass and feel of a wet sandbag. I took two steps to the side as I regained my balance. The thing's own weight worked against it, and it fell back and toppled heavily over a tree root.

They were strong but not light on their feet. As another one loomed ahead, I feinted to go around it first right, then left. It clumsily followed, and I seized it by the shoulders and gave it a powerful heave that continued the movement and overbalanced it into what was almost a cartwheel.

Even then, I was thinking of the fight in the Knyght's Head and the tricky calculus of how many opponents there were, how far away they were, how quickly I could knock them down, and how long it would take them to get to their feet. Unless I was very swift indeed, I was going to get bogged down with fighting again.

I managed another three paces forward before my way was blocked by a smaller figure, the remnant perhaps of a woman or a child. It felt very much like a heavy punching bag to my fist, and while it flailed back, it lacked the speed or reach to connect with me. My blows, which should have felled a full-grown man, seemed to have no effect. I increased the power, and on the sixth or seventh strike to its torso, it folded and fell away as though something inside had broken.

Skinner was on his knees by that point. Two of the creatures had dragged him to the pool, and as one of them held his arms, the other forced his head down under the surface of the water.

I was knocked down by something pale and bulky, which came at me from one side. The blow had been pure chance, but it had the force of a battering ram. I rolled and got up to see a creature with a torso the size of a barrel looming over me. I did not look closely at it—I was careful to avoid looking at any of them—but I had the impression it was composed of three or more bodies mashed together as though their flesh was modelling clay. The ogrish form looked about and raised a thick arm towards me like a blind man feeling his way. Its hands were like rough spades.

Punching that monster would have been like striking a cliff face. Without hesitation, I threw the translucent yellow-brown pellet at it.

I expected the projectile to bounce off or maybe shatter, but instead, it merged with the creature as though they were both made of liquid. The effect was as though I had thrown a match on a scarecrow soaked in kerosene—there was a pulse of light, and the glow the pellet emitted suddenly burned a hundred times brighter, breaking into purple-and-black flames. The creature burned where it stood, writhing like burning paper. The flame was fierce as though gas jets were erupting from every inch of its body.

There was no heat that I could feel; all the energy was turned inwards, tearing the creature's fabric into dust and smoke. It disintegrated as fast as if it had been a hollow figure made of dry newspaper.

I sensed rather than saw more of them zigzagging nearby. Another bulky figure even bigger than the last crashed through the undergrowth, heading straight at me. I sidestepped his charge easily, dodging behind the trunk of a tree, and tapped his ankle as he passed. He stumbled, missed his step, and went down heavily into a patch of brambles.

I strode over to where two great hulks with human form held Skinner down. They were like sinister faceless mannequins. Skinner's head was fully submerged, but he still struggled feebly. Drawing in my breath, I focused my energies into a single point. I knew a secret blow that could break a wooden plank; I would never have used it on a human opponent even without a knuckleduster. But this was a life-or-death situation. Without hesitation or thought, my fist flew as I delivered the secret Chinese blow, taught to me by Yang, to the head of the attacker holding Skinner's face under water.

The thing's head crumbled at the impact like a clod of hard earth under a sledgehammer. Its decapitated body fell away as the fragments pattered into the water.

Skinner raised his face from the pool, gasping. Luminous water streamed from his hair.

I kicked the shoulder of the one holding Skinner's arms. That should have broken some bones. In any event, it was enough to make the thing loosen its grip and turn around. As it tried to stand, I pivoted and kicked it in the chest, hard enough to leave a footprint, and it toppled back, its chest caved in.

Skinner squirmed free, splashing and staggering through the water. Another figure approached, but I knocked it down with a well-timed straight right. Their balance was as poor as if they walked on stilts.

We fled. They tried to stop us, but the big ones were not agile enough, and the smaller ones were not strong enough or quick enough to hold us. Neither their clutches nor the ever-entangling undergrowth was a match for our desperation to escape, and we pelted blindly back the way we had come.

Away from the soft light of the oak, the darkness was complete, and it was like plunging into the warm embrace of a friendly ocean lit only by Skinner's torch, shining the way ahead.

Our pursuers were not following the path but wading through the undergrowth. That slowed them but not by as much as I would have liked. As we approached the junction with the main path, I glimpsed something white ahead—a self-luminous man crawling along the ground, or attempting to crawl. He was caught up in the barbed wire, and his progress was hampered by the object that he carried tucked under one arm like a rugby ball.

The circle of the torchlight captured his upturned face. Pierce was barely recognisable in the degenerated features, but I knew it was him. The gardener had succeeded in stealing the idol and had made it this far, but his body was crumbling away. He was utterly spent. That was why the first of those alien undead had emerged from the earth—not to attack us, but to retrieve the idol.

"We'll take that." Skinner reached out with both hands, and bronze gleamed as he gently pulled the idol from under Pierce's arm. Pierce was too weak to stop him but babbled at us as if several voices were trying to speak to us at once. Then the other voices subsided, and Pierce clutched my trouser cuff and spoke to me in a near whisper.

"They're not devils," he croaked. "They're angels, fallen from heaven. Tell Evie. Tell her I've gone to heaven."

The pursuers were crashing through the wood, a skirmish line of them beating their way and searching through the undergrowth. There seemed to be more of them now.

"Leave him," urged Skinner.

I was thinking fast, putting together everything I had seen and heard—Stafford's idea of the Holy Grail against Miss De Vere's warning of alien infection, of lightning bolts and burning caravans, the colony of lepers put to the sword in Africa. I thought of the reason why they had encased the meteorite in metal in the first place. They must have wanted to preserve it in one piece so it could be transported.

"No," I said. "We have to give it back to them."

Skinner looked at me, dumbfounded, holding the idol in both hands. This was the prize that Stafford and Miss De Vere wanted and the only coin that Elsie Granger would accept for Sally's safe return, but it did not belong to any of them.

Then he grinned. Perhaps, if he still had his knife and if I had not just saved him, he would have done differently. Skinner always said I should not trust him. But he grinned, enjoying the joke of it all.

"Why not?" he said and passed it to me.

The idol was as Miss Horniman had described it, and though the metal was smooth and slippery, I pulled the two halves apart in an instant.

The stone inside glowed as though it had been painted with radium. It was the size of a coconut and marked with ridges and pits as though pieces had been gouged from it. It was warm to the touch, and though it was heavy enough, it did not feel like a stone at all but more like a living thing, so yielding that I thought I could leave an impression with my finger. It might have been the cocoon of a monstrous insect.

Skinner gaped when he saw it, but I did not pause to look at the stone. That would be a bad mistake. Looking at things like that always was a mistake. That our brains were not equipped to assimilate some things was a truth I was beginning to appreciate, and being in mortal danger was not a good state for your mind to bite off more than it could chew.

I threw the baetyl with all my force back through the woods, towards the twisted oak. It vanished into the night. I could not hear it land because of the racket made by our pursuers, but a second later, silence fell suddenly over the forest.

"What now?" asked Skinner.

"Now we wait." I wanted to ask Skinner whether he had swallowed any water. Still, there was nothing I could do if he had, and we would find out soon enough.

I shone a light on Pierce's body. I could not identify a pulse, but I was convinced that he was not dead, or at least no deader than he had been a minute before—though he was probably not truly alive when he spoke his last words.

The air tingled as before an electrical storm. I was expecting thunderbolts, but none came. Instead, there was crackling from inside the woods like a bonfire and odd sparks of floating light that came and went. The popping and crackling rose and became continuous.

Something barrelled down the path towards us. I tensed, and my torch briefly shone in the terrified eyes of a fox before it bounded off, away from the pale, phosphorescent gyre that was climbing higher and higher into the sky.

At first, I thought it must be a forest fire, but the lights were not flames. They were more clusters of fireflies, whole squadrons of them, armadas of them. Every single animal and plant that was infected was crumbling into dust, yielding up its energies, and the pool must have boiled with strange light as the last vestiges were released from the subterranean pores.

"Like cosmic blooming carnival lights," said Skinner.

The Northern Lights have been described as sheets and curtains of light which writhe across the night sky, and perhaps that was what we saw under the forest canopy. Or perhaps it was more like the electrical St Elmo's fire that Captain Hall spoke of so vividly, crawling along the masthead and the rigging, seemingly made of living light. The light certainly clung to the branches like rainwater. There was a sense of rotation too. The light was all caught up in a whirlpool or was creating a whirlpool itself, one that pulled itself up above the trees.

There was a sigh from my feet. A pale trickle of light flowed up towards the oak like a luminous eel. As it left Pierce, his body seethed and crumbled into dust. His body was surely dead, but as for the rest of him… if the essence of an alien being could move from a meteorite into water then into human flesh and back again into pure light, then perhaps some portion of a human being might make the same transition. As that flicker vanished into the woods, perhaps it really did take his soul with it. Bound, Pierce seemed sure, for heaven.

"What have we done?" asked Skinner quietly. "What have we done?"

The crackling had grown so much by then that it was like the rushing of a waterfall, pure white noise, not loud but overwhelming, coming from everywhere at once.

The gyre had expanded, ballooning out towards us so it seemed close enough to touch. The surface was covered in crazy shifting patterns, some of them like leaves or branches, some like animal forms, and some, half glimpsed, like human faces. It spun faster and then extended upwards into a tall, narrow vortex.

The rotating cylinder climbed up itself, like ivy clambering over ivy, reaching upwards in waves. Twice it surged up only to slump down again. Each time, the light seemed to fade, but the third wave rolled upwards and upwards, extending high into the sky. The peak latched onto or bore through something as though some level of the firmament really was made of solid crystal. For a moment, the entire cyclone pulsed electric blue and thrummed as it drank deep from a fountain of lightning and replenished its energy.

Then the whole huge, whirling mass catapulted upwards, becoming a dart, a flaming arrow shot into the heavens, a shooting star passing out beyond the moon and vanishing in an eye-blink. We were left in darkness.

The after-image left me blinded for a minute. The noise in the woods did not die down at once but gradually faded as everything settled back into place after the big oak tree had finally become dust, branches, trunk, and roots, and the pool had disappeared back into the cavity.

"It's gone," I said at last.

"I bloody well hope so," said Skinner.

Chapter Eighteen

Unfinished Business

Next day, Sunday morning, I walked into Norwood New Town at Arthur Renville's side. There were no police on the gate, but it still had the feel of a prison camp. A deserted one. Everyone was sleeping off Saturday night.

"What a beautiful day," said Arthur. He walked down the street as though he owned the place, or at least was considering putting in an offer. "God's in his heaven, and all's right with the world, wouldn't you say, Stubbsy?"

Arthur was a happy man. He had secured a large consignment of cigarettes, written off as waterlogged, and had confirmed that the majority were of a saleable quality. The night before, he had been busy ensuring that boxes and boxes of cigarettes all found secure homes, which was not an easy thing with a negotiable commodity such as tobacco. He would be going to bed in an hour or two.

I made some noncommittal reply.

"Don't you worry." He patted my arm. "We'll get everything sorted out here."

When I had come to Arthur, I had half expected he'd get on the blower and assemble an army to descend on Norwood New Town mob-handed with pick-axe handles for weapons. But he had insisted that the two of us would be more than enough.

Arthur was a friendly, reassuring presence. If he said the sun would shine tomorrow, you knew it was so. If Skinner said the same thing, you would still wonder about taking an umbrella.

Skinner had gone as soon as the events in the forest were

concluded. From the woods, he had headed directly to the fairground with just the clothes he wore and the money in his pocket. He wanted me to go with him.

"Nobody cares about your name or your past in a fair," he said. "Nobody asks to see your papers. You disappear. And there's plenty a chap like you could do—you'd be a first-class strongman act. Shave your head and grow a beard, and nobody would recognise you. You'd do well enough as a mucker—you could do the work of three other blokes. But if you go back, your life ain't worth a bent farthing; you know that."

I had turned him down, not without regrets. While Skinner could run away, I needed to face up to things, not the least of which was Sally's kidnapping.

The Knyght's Head was closed and shuttered with no sign of life. Arthur strolled around to the side door, listened for a minute, and then rapped on it twice.

After a minute, a boy opened the door wide enough to look suspiciously at us. He was about half my height with dishevelled hair and a stained shirt several sizes too big for his undersized frame. He waited for us to speak.

"Would you be so good as to give this to Miss Elsie?" said Arthur, passing a business card through the narrow opening. "We'll be at the front door when she's ready."

Having taken the card, the boy shut the door again. We sauntered back to the front. The place had the aspect of a bunker. Broken glass crunched underfoot. The side door opened again, and I heard running feet. The boy had been sent on an errand.

"A very fine morning," Arthur repeated, gazing into the cloudless sky. "Look, you can see the swallows flying up there."

Five minutes later, there were more footsteps around at the side door; the summoned reinforcements had arrived. Shortly afterwards, the front door opened, and Elsie Granger herself stood inside with arms folded, squinting into the bright sun.

"You were told to bring it," she grated.

"I think we need to have a discussion," said Arthur. "Shall we go inside, or would you like to come out here?"

She ushered us in. There were men standing in the shadows at the back of the room. I took three stools down from the tables, and we sat in the empty pub. It was smaller than I remembered.

Elsie was wearing her fancy barmaid's dress but with a shawl over it as though it was not quite proper in the light of day.

"And what have you got to say for yourselves?" Her arms were still crossed, but Arthur's appearance had made some impression. She must have heard his name, and she could never have seen anyone of his calibre in the establishment. While he was not intimidating, Arthur could be formidable. He always said that he was merely a figurehead, not a captain, but in practice, he had at his command a large and powerful organisation that occupied the area around the New Town, completely surrounding it.

"I don't think we need be hostile to one another, Miss Granger," Arthur said mildly. "I was hoping to do business with you on amiable terms. I wanted to start by saying how very impressed I am at your operation here."

"Oh, yes," she said with a barmaid's immunity to flattery.

"This place has been nothing but chaos for as long as anyone can remember." Arthur's gesture took in the whole New Town area, but he might have been talking about the pub, which showed marks of violence and neglect. "Not just without law but lawless, if you get my meaning. Everybody was at each other's throats and in each other's pockets. Nobody ever managed to get them organised before, but you did, and for that, I salute you. Once you get them organised, you can do anything. You can build something. Make some real money."

A sidelong look suggested she was not entirely uninterested.

"Now to brass tacks. As you may not know, the object which you seek is no more." Arthur waved a hand as if dispersing smoke. "Mr Stubbs is in no position to give it to you. And he did us all a great service by getting rid of it."

"It doesn't help me," she grumbled.

"Oh, but it does. Furthermore, even if we were to let you have it… the prospective buyer is also no longer with us."

"What?" Her eyes narrowed.

After parting with Skinner, I had gone from the woods to the Firs. I knew that Stafford would want to know what had occurred. I did not know how he would react, and I cherished a hope, albeit a faint one, that he might be pleased with the outcome.

I had expected the Firs to be dark and quiet, but every window was lit up, and servants rushed about. There was a car in the driveway, and two women were sobbing outside the front door.

The butler, in his shirtsleeves, stopped to talk to me. It seemed that Stafford had been working that evening in his observatory and had rushed out in a state of high excitement. There was a display of summer lightning towards Beulah Hill, and he had brought the whole household out on to the lawn to see it, some of them in their nightclothes.

As they watched the atmospheric lights, Stafford had become incoherent, talking to them about transfiguration and apotheosis. The butler would not disclose details, but I could imagine his employer's mystical frenzy. Just before the climax, Stafford had gone into convulsions and died.

"Did anything unusual happen just before he died? Or just after?"

"I really couldn't say, sir," said the butler.

"Was a there a coloured light –" I started. The butler's face was blank, shuttered. What he had seen he would carry to the grave. But I was convinced that an autopsy would have found part of Stafford's brain—the part where his deepest self resided—melted to powder. "Never mind. None of it matters now."

"Will that be all, sir?"

"Yes. No, just one thing. Do you have a housemaid called Evie working here? I'm supposed to give her a message."

The butler reluctantly conceded that there might be a young person of that name in the establishment. I wrote out what Pierce had said on a sheet from my notebook and gave it to the butler. I did not want to deliver the message face-to-face.

"Very good, sir." The butler hesitated a moment and cleared his throat. "Does the, ah, settlement of your accounts require a final payment from Mr Stafford?"

There was a world of implication in those words. The butler knew some of the details of our employment. Perhaps he knew what Skinner was like. If he could save the estate any heartache and future claims connected with "Lantern Insurance," it would be well worth paying for our silence.

"Oh, no," I said. "Mr Stafford paid for everything. And—my sincere condolences to you all."

"Very good, sir," he repeated.

He'd actually bowed to me before turning to go back into the house.

Stafford's death was the closing of a door. With him went the last hope of assistance from a person of influence, one who understood about the baetyl. All that was left was my old friend and mentor, Arthur Renville. I had found him in a stable yard piled with crates. Luckily for me, Arthur's night's work was at an end, and he was able to give me a hearing. And there we were.

"Mr Stafford passed away last night of natural causes," Arthur told Elsie. "He won't be buying anything from anyone." He let the words sink in a moment. "All of which leaves any discussion of the item in question as having no practical value."

Elsie did not miss a beat. "So what have you got to offer me instead? Assuming you want to see *her* again."

"I have taken a personal interest in Sally's wellbeing," said Arthur in the same mild tone. "She is a good woman who has been through hard times—there but for the grace of God go all of us! Her late husband worked for me, and I would take it amiss if anything was to happen to her. But as I said, I was favourably impressed by the way you've brought order here. This operation is proof positive that you've got the place organised at last. I think you have the necessary underpinning to join in a rather lucrative venture."

"So you have got something to trade."

He had her interest now.

Arthur outlined briefly the essentials of the consignment business, of the need for plenty of reliable hands to transport and store goods, to deliver them to customers, and to collect and distribute payment. It was like any other business, but the handling of money was on a more informal basis, and though the letter of the rules was loose, the enforcement of the spirit could be harsh.

"The enterprise relies on having trustworthy men at every link in the chain so there's no pilferage or diversion," said Arthur. "It's like an electric circuit: only if every connection is sound can money flow from one end to the other."

"If I wanted to sell odds and ends," she said, "I'd get myself a market stall."

"Our current consignment is one of cigarettes," said Arthur, placing a pack on the table in front of her with a box of matches on top of it. "Quite decent ones, as it happens. You'll have plenty of takers at this price."

Elsie looked at the cigarettes and tossed the box to the men slouched at the bar. "How many are you trying to get rid of?"

"How many do you think you can handle in a week?" he parried.

"Depends how much you're asking for each pack."

A quick-fire discussion followed. Both of them showed off their ability to do mental arithmetic, and they ended up quibbling amiably over the difference a farthing could make. Elsie's voice had dropped low. The previous discussion was meant to be shared with her crew, but she had no intention of letting anyone else in on the exact terms of the business arrangement.

She broke off once to ask the boys if the cigarettes were any good and received a chorus of approval.

"You're not expecting cash up front," she said.

"Not a bit of it," said Arthur. "Your word is good enough for me, Miss Granger. You can pay me whenever you should find it convenient, within the fortnight."

Her eyes shifted rapidly as though reading a legal contract and looking for the catch. "You're asking to get robbed. Goods up front and no payment?"

"Strangely enough," said Arthur, looking her straight in the eye, "everybody always pays up. I like to think I'm a good judge of character."

"It helps if you've got a few like him," she said, indicating me. "He's a right brawler."

"Oh, no," said Arthur, "Mr Stubbs is one of a kind. And I'm not in favour of brawling. But I think you appreciate more than most the finer points of the business."

The conversation had become more relaxed, and they were soon talking shop like old friends. Arthur had little intelligence about what went on inside the confines of the New Town and was particularly interested in how often the police visited. I think he saw the Knyght's Head as a prospective free-trade zone outside of the reach of customs and excise, like a miniature Singapore that would attract business from far and wide.

Their conversation was soon ranging wider. Elsie had little knowledge of matters outside of the New Town and knew of Arthur's world only by rumour, and Arthur knew little more about goings-on in the New Town. Each was eager to find out what the other knew about various individuals and their activities, robberies, assaults, and disappearances.

I must have shifted impatiently, because Arthur looked around and noticed me again.

"Now I think of it," said Arthur, "perhaps Mr Stubbs could escort Sally home while we continue our private conversation."

Elsie turned around and barked at her crew. "Adam! Bring her out front, and let her go." The ferret-faced man slouched into an upright position, sucking on a cigarette. "Today, if you please!" Elsie added.

"That's very good of you," said Arthur. "I'm much obliged. Do give Sally my compliments, Stubbsy, and see you make it up to her. Perhaps you could take her to lunch with your folks as it's Sunday."

"I'm in your debt yet again," I said.

Elsie was already asking Arthur about a certain corrupt police inspector who had been troubling her.

Two of the toughs escorted Sally into the street. She was taller than they were, and she walked like a queen, anything but cowed. She did not seem much the worse for wear. I was surprised, then, when she fell into my arms and clung to me.

"Harry!" she said, in a choked voice only I could hear. "I knew you'd come."

"There, there," I said.

"No hard feelings," her escort, Adam, said over Sally's shoulder. He was standing at a safe enough distance from me just in case I took offence. I could see the cut on his face that Skinner had inflicted.

"None at all," I assured him.

I took Sally's arm, and we walked down the deserted street and out the gate that led into the recreation ground.

"I was scared at first," she said. "Only a little bit, though. It didn't take long to see through them. They were more scared than I was. You could see they'd never done a kidnapping before—they didn't even have a proper blindfold!"

"Did they hurt you?"

"Not much," she said matter-of-factly. "A few bruises. Nothing I haven't had before and ten times worse. They stuck me in a broom closet that smelled of mouse droppings, with two of them on guard outside. I thought, two of them? Who do they think I am, Houdini? So I just curled up and went to sleep."

"You were very brave."

"What about you though?" she asked suddenly. "What happened last night?"

I gave her an abbreviated version of the events in the forest. I was just explaining how Skinner had gone off when Sally tugged my arm urgently. "Here's trouble," she said.

A powder-blue limousine glided to a halt a few feet away, the rear window already sliding down.

Miss De Vere looked out with all the expression of a sphinx. I could not detect anger or malice or any other human emotion in her beautiful face. She might have been posing for a photograph.

"Hello," said Sally politely. "It's nice to see you again, Estelle."

"I didn't know you two were friends," said Miss De Vere, deadpan. "If you'll excuse me, perhaps I can take Mr Stubbs away from you for a minute?"

Sally started to say that we were on our way somewhere, but I stepped into the car. There was no point in trying to run.

The interior was shadowy and felt chilly after the sunny street, as though Miss De Vere emanated cold. She was wearing a long dress of black, lacy material, with a hat on her lap. A tiny gold crucifix, with a diamond at each point, set off the outfit.

A cigarette in an ebony holder glowed in her gloved hand.

Her exhalation looked like breath on a frosty day. I wondered if her other hand, under the hat, was holding a weapon—assuming she needed one.

The scene flickered just for an instant. For that moment, we were in a deep chamber far beneath the surface of the earth. I had the faint impression of figures chained to bare rock walls, of armed guards lurking in the shadows, but before I could fully grasp it, the image had gone. The impression was clear enough, though.

I had already considered this exact situation and whether simply attacking Miss De Vere would be my best form of self-defence. I had concluded that it would be foolish, and that while she might seem to be a slight and vulnerable woman, any assault I could mount was likely to be futile.

Miss De Vere spoke less languidly and more forcefully than before. If she was angry, she kept it in check.

"You found the place. You didn't do what you were supposed to do. Care to tell me what happened?"

"I don't believe I ever was in your employment," I said carefully.

"True," she said, tapping ash into the chrome ashtray built into an armrest. "Technically."

"Perhaps we can trade information between us."

I had been encouraged by how well Arthur had got along with Elsie Granger. Where there was a common interest, there was always room for an accommodation.

She regarded me for a long moment.

"The arrangement works like this," she said softly. "I can have you, or any member of your family, killed before Sunday lunch. Or I could have you jailed for your involvement in any one of—how many?—unexplained deaths. You might have information, but you have—and please correct me if I'm wrong—precisely nothing to negotiate with. Ergo, I ask the questions."

She pronounced the Latin word as "air-go."

My scalp prickled. Few people could deliver a threat effectively. Miss De Vere could have given classes. Her slow, calm delivery was remarkably effective.

I was not, however, an easy man to bully. My insurance

policy—these written chapters that explain what had happened and who was involved—would be next to useless. It might in fact be a liability, revealing too much of what I knew and implicating Hoade and Sally to boot. I had assumed that Latham and Rowe would not give up the manuscript to anyone without my say-so, but Miss De Vere's powers were formidable, and perhaps she would find her way to it—if she knew of its existence. So I decided not to reveal it.

But I still had a few cards to play.

"I don't know exactly what happened to Mabel Brown," I said. "Judging from subsequent events, I'm inclined to believe that you were responsible. But I'm not sure why you killed her without getting the baetyl."

She raised one eyebrow. Then after a moment, she answered. "We were getting on fine, Mabel and I. Once we had both understood that she knew I knew she had it, the only question was where it was. Unfortunately... she said something dumb."

"What was that?"

"She told me she'd swallowed it."

"She thought that would stop you from searching her room. But as far as you were concerned, it meant she was dangerously contaminated."

"That's a good word," she said, pretending to be impressed. "So... I decontaminated her."

She blew a slow jet of smoke.

"With an alchemical incendiary mixture. Like the one you gave me."

"It's isomeric," she said. "I'll let you look that one up."

"You burned Madam Hester's caravan the same way."

"She was a gipsy," said Miss De Vere as though that both explained and excused it. "We had a rather short conversation. She tried to kill me. Another dumb decision."

"You talk about not opening Pandora's box, but you dip into it yourself when you feel like it."

Her smile was almost a smirk. Even then, her features were flawless. Almost inhumanly flawless, when you looked closely.

"Sometimes the Theral Development Society fights fire with fire," she said without a trace of guilt.

"But Miss Horniman is still alive," I said. "And the others from the Golden Dawn."

"Poseurs," she said. "But so entertaining. Willie Yeats is a real charmer. The more theatrical types there are performing weird ceremonies in purple robes, the better. They're not... dangerous."

She looked up at me from under her eyelashes.

Did she mean that I was dangerous? Perhaps I had miscalculated. But I had nowhere to go except forward. "It wasn't coincidence that the spring started up again or that Stafford saw the periodic body. It is like a ship dropping off boats. The ship had returned, and the boats went out to meet it. But they needed to have all hands to man the oars, and that's why all the pieces had to come together. It just wanted to get back where it came from. I think you knew that."

She looked displeased at the crude simile. No doubt the real science was much more exact and I was mangling the truth, but I was convinced I was close enough.

"I told you it might have turned this place into a wasteland, and you didn't stop it," she said, shaking her head at my stupidity. "You helped it. You think it's like a friendly lion with its paw in a trap? That it'll thank you for helping it next time you meet? No. No. It's alien. It doesn't even recognise humans."

I was not so sure about that. I thought it had some understanding. That was why it tried to force Skinner into the pool—not to drown him but to get him to drink and become part of it. But it was as careless of individual humans as we were of toenail clippings.

"As long as it stayed here, it would harm people. That's why it had to go back."

That really was what it came down to. Of course, I would never know what happened to Stafford and Pierce and the others. Did Stafford achieve the mystical communion with a celestial being that he yearned for? Did Pierce really ascend with angels to merge with some astral heaven even as his body disintegrated?

Miss De Vere's view was that their brains had been infected with alien parasites and their opinions counted for nothing. I was much less sure. I could not even imagine what fusing with a greater being might entail or whether it could be desirable. A poet wrote about becoming "a pulse in the eternal mind" as though it was a good thing. Was being absorbed a horrible death or a form of blissful immortality?

I was less sure of anything than Miss De Vere and had nobody to advise me. But faced with such an unknown situation, the safest thing was to try and keep things as they were, without alien forces. So in a sense, we were of the same opinion. But I did not think that her straightforward physical interpretation was much better than the religious and mythical framework that Stafford tried to shoehorn his experiences into. Neither was willing to accept how much they did not know, and they filled the gaps with their own angels and monsters.

"Very smart," she said sarcastically. "Know what you've done? You've let their scout get back with intelligence about our world. Now it has everything Stafford and Pierce and the others knew."

"I don't think it was a scout. I think it was a collector. Like Mr Horniman, collecting his beetles and butterflies from exotic places. It wants to collect samples of everything. It didn't even occur to Horniman to think that he was doing harm, and I don't think the alien knows, either. The piece of it that landed here was like a deep-sea diver sent to collect exotic specimens and then go back. It can't survive here; it just crumbles away when it tries to take on a form."

What I really wanted to say was that it was a librarian. Hoade was proud of his collection of books but not so mindful of the people who read them. And like him, the alien was not so interested in amassing objects as in collecting information and taking it back to some cosmic brain.

The meteorite itself was something like ballast, allowing the visitor to get down to the surface. The visitor could move from one physical medium to another; its essence was intangible. I had guessed as much on the day the lightning struck. The alien visitor was like a tune that existed on a piece of sheet music and became a set of vibrations when the pianist read the notation, which might then be turned into radio waves and back into sound waves or be captured in the grooves on a gramophone record. The tune itself survived all those changes unharmed even if you burned the original sheet music.

What had returned to space had been entirely nonphysical. All it took from our world was information, knowledge, and experience—and, as Miss De Vere seemed to confirm, something of the minds of the humans it had contacted. I remembered the cyclone of images—a glimpse, perhaps, of its memory.

Perhaps it was like a galactic library or a gigantic Horniman Museum or even its own version of Everett's freak show. Whatever it was, I was convinced that the motive was curiosity and not conquest. A nonphysical being would not want gold, like the Spanish conquistadores, or land or other physical booty. Just knowledge.

"Scout, collector—that's semantics," she said. "Anything that comes down here has to die, period."

"If you saw them, I don't know if you'd be so confident you could stop them."

"Try me," she said.

I told her about the scene at the pool, of the many bodies that crawled and slithered out of the ground, and of our struggle. That tiny line appeared between her brows again. I did not mention either the star stone or the secret blow that Yang had taught me, without which the encounter might have ended very differently. She must have been calculating whether I could have survived without help and what sort of help it could have been.

"If we had tried to run away with the idol, there might have been dozens of them after us, and I don't know what else." What had she called it? *A million fragments, discontinuous but cohesive*—perhaps cohesive enough to eventually bring all its elements to bear on us, including myriad crawling and flying things. If it wanted to raise a battalion, how long would it have taken to drag unsuspecting householders from their porches and force them to drink from the pool?

"I don't know how far we would have got," I went on. "And in such a heavily populated area, a lot of people might have been caught in the middle."

She sighed and looked out the window. "Christ almighty. You do realise, Stubbs, don't you, that you can't fight a war without breaking eggs?"

"There would also have been a large number of witnesses. The police would certainly have been involved. And the government afterwards."

That irritated her too, but perhaps she was more irritated with herself than with me. There was a long silence as I waited for her to speak.

"Anyway," she said at last, seeming to brighten. "The contamination is gone. There's no risk of it spreading any farther. Nobody is going to sell any more nuggets or drink anything they shouldn't. And Stafford is out of the picture… maybe we just need a small fire in his library to be sure."

I suspected the alternative was burning the whole place down. I held my tongue.

"And a few other loose ends. Where is Skinner?" she asked.

"I don't know. He's gone."

"Of course he has," she said, amused. "As fast and as far as his little feet will carry him. Maybe I won't send the hounds after him, if he lies low and keeps his trap shut. He's smart. He got his fingers burned once, and he's had enough. But what about you?"

There was something about the way she asked that question, the little smile at the corners of her mouth. I was in her power, and she wanted me to know it. But I was not about to beg for mercy.

"I don't know," I said.

"You… are ridiculous. You want to fight extraterrestrials with your fists, and your correspondence course in detective work? It's pathetic. You haven't got a clue. You don't even have a gun."

I doubted whether a blazing six-gun in each hand would have stood me in any stead against those pale, unhuman things. And I knew when I was being baited. I saw no reason to apologise for my methods or my results.

"In the jargon of your national sport," I said slowly, "I'm batting three for three. I'll stand by that record."

"Three for three, huh?" There was something disturbing in her gaze. It was not just that she hated me, though I was sure she did. There was something more than that. Somehow, I represented something she wanted but had never found. There was desire in her look... she looked at me as though I were food.

I was the one who looked away first.

"We'll see how your batting average goes when you're working for me," she said.

That was the real reason I was still alive and she had not turned me over to the police, as she no doubt could have done. We were, after all, broadly on the same side. And while I was not technically working for her, and the outcome had not been what she had desired, I had already been loosely working on her team.

It was inevitable that she would view me as being either an ally or an enemy. Those who knew as much as I did must either be part of the organisation or be eliminated. Skinner had understood that.

I considered the matter, and I felt that a working arrangement might be possible as long as I was given a degree of independence. Whether I could mitigate her excesses or we would come to blows was another question.

"Alternatively..." I ventured.

"Believe me, there is no 'alternatively.'"

"I see," I said.

She reached out and touched my damaged ear. "Maybe we can do something about this." Her gloved fingers were cool.

"I don't know," I said, trying not to shy away.

"Maybe I'll put in a good word, and you'll get a raise," she said, enjoying my discomfiture. "Danger money."

"Thank you."

"Welcome to the cormorant fishing business." She winked. "You'll get your orders in due course. I believe I have your address."

"I can write it down if you like."

She contemplated me for a moment longer, like the new pet owner considering a dog that looked sound but might still require some training.

"Goodbye, Stubbs," she said, putting her hand on the lever that opened the car door. "I have to flirt with a bishop."

"Good morning, Miss De Vere." I stepped out into dazzling daylight.

I had survived, but the world was a darker place. My friend Skinner was gone, and I was deeply entangled with people who were no less dangerous than the alien influences they resisted with such ferocity. Conflict seemed inevitable, and my life or death might depend on Miss De Vere's whim.

Even on a clear day, meteorites rained down like hailstones, invisible in the summer sky, each an emissary from an alien star and bearing an unknown cargo. Some were harmless or perhaps even benign; some were burning brands. Miss De Vere's circle was determined to stamp on all of them before they could spread, and stamp on anyone they deemed to be contaminated. And I was now part of the struggle.

Sally, who had been sitting at a bench down the street, stood up as she saw me. It was not quite full summer. There was the faintest breeze, and already, I felt a diminution of the sun's power. Perhaps it was only because I was so fatigued, but the weather seemed a little less warm than the day before. For the first time, I thought I sensed the inevitable approach of autumn in the air.

Editor's Note

As usual, Harry Stubbs's account is consistent with the known facts, as far as they can be checked.

Annie Horniman was a friend and supporter of W. B. Yeats and bought the Abbey Theatre in Dublin for his nascent group of Irish playwrights. It was her patronage that secured Liddell Mathers much-needed work at her father's museum. The collection was originally housed in the Hornimans' family home, which it eventually outgrew. Annie Horniman was prone to arguments with those close to her. She split with Mathers in 1896—due to a disagreement over "marriages" with elemental beings—and did not talk to Yeats after 1909. She broke with her family in 1897 when her father remarried.

Paracelsus does mention *"Necrocomica"* in his work, referring to some type of meteor. The word is of obscure origin and is one of his many coinages. Paracelsus also originated the words *zinc*—he discovered the metal—*alcohol,* which is possibly derived from the Arabic, and *gnome.* He made an inspection of the Ennisheim meteorite, still on display in modern times, which he did not consider to be miraculous.

There are no reliable records of Paracelsus writing a *Liber Necrocomicon.* He did, however, write a large number of scientific, medical, prophetic, and mystical works, many of which were not published until after his death. Heretical or other dangerous writings might have been kept secret, and collectors tend to hoard rare manuscripts, so a text may yet emerge—though other works have been falsely attributed to Paracelsus. The task of compiling a definitive bibliography will keep scholars occupied for some centuries more.

The debate over *panspermia* and the possibility of microorganisms or diseases being carried by meteorites continues. Scientific evidence remains scant, although there is a rich folklore, such as that surrounding the mysterious outbreak in New England in 1882, which inspired H. P. Lovecraft's *"The Colour Out of Space."*

About the Author

David Hambling is a journalist and author who has lived in Norwood, South London since 2000. He writes about science and technology for New Scientist magazine, The Economist, WIRED, Popular Mechanics, and writes a science column for Fortean Times ("the magazine of unexplained phenomena"). In addition to non-fiction books, his "Shadows From Norwood" project seeks to bring HP Lovecraft's Cthulhu Mythos to South London, via the Harry Stubbs novels and a number of short stories.

Visit the Shadows from Norwood Facebook page :

https://www.facebook.com/ShadowsFromNorwood

...for links, photographs, interactive map and more about the Harry Stubbs Adventures series